Knowing When To Leave

by

Vin Morreale, Jr.

Edited by Rebecca Prem Groppe

Cover Design by Susan Coleman Layman

ISBN 978-0-9991473-1-3

academyartspress.com

TABLE OF CONTENTS

TABLE OF CONTENTS

What pitiable things
We mortals be
Who long for love
Yet lose and leave
With wretched regularity

THE STARS AND THE UPHOLSTERY

There were depressingly frequent flecks of grey in her hair and in her soul, as her anxious eyes danced around the stiflingly comfortable room; the oversized clock, faded hummingbird wallpaper, the mocking photos of happier times, the furniture, as frayed and worn as she felt inside, until her gaze, as always, fell back to the achingly familiar stranger sharing her sofa. The one she struggled so desperately to remain in love with for far longer than she cared to remember.

As always, Charlie and Belinda Caldwell sat perched on opposite ends of the old sofa, an intimidating expanse of frayed flowered upholstery between them. Belinda's crossed knees pressed against her chosen arm of the couch, just as Charlie's flannel-covered elbow leaned upon his. Together they stared silently at that marvel of modern communication, the big-screen television set. Lost in this world of shared isolation, they blinked only with their eyes and spoke only between commercials, which were far too frequent for comfort. At random intervals, Charlie would raise the sleek, black remote control, which occupied his hand from the first moment he plopped heavily down, exhausted from the demands of the day. They would each focus intently on the screen as it shuttled between laugh tracks and melodramas, crime and knowledge, music and mayhem; a manic minuet of compulsive channel surfing in an elusive search for something to crack the boredom.

"Hey," Belinda said, without removing her eyes from the screen. A documentary on insect larvae flew past, followed quickly by a casual murder, an overly enthusiastic daytime host, and a well-known comedy, still void of humor after more than three decades in reruns.

"Hey. I said 'hey'."

"So what?" Charlie shrugged. "Hey don't mean nothin'."

"I was just trying to get your attention is all."

"Well, you got it," he grumbled, pressing the channel button on the remote again. An infomercial chortled and gushed over the miraculous benefits of spray-on hair in a can. This was where the remote rested for a while, Charlie and Belinda retreating to the numbing comfort of the unsatisfyingly mundane. After a moment, she spoke again.

"Can't you do anything but watch TV when you get home?" she said finally.

"Can't you do anything but bitch about what I can and can't do?"

She turned to glare at him. "I don't bitch, Charlie. You can't say I bitch. I point out quirks, is all."

"Quirks, she says!" Charlie snorted without humor. "Quirks. That's a good one."

"What's the matter? You don't think you got quirks?"

He turned to her for the first time, his voice raised in angry defense. "Listen, Lady. I got quirks. I got plenty of quirks!"

"You're telling me…" Belinda shrugged in the manner she knew would irritate him the most. It worked.

"I already said I got quirks, okay?! You don't have to keep pointing them out all the time. It don't make them go away." He raised the remote control, and hurtled them through space, through jungles, through other people's living rooms, and finally into an animated forest infested with talking animals.

"You got quirks, too, you know," he added.

"I know I got quirks. Everybody's got quirks…." Belinda said, and they both fell silent until a corpulent man interrupted the children's show with a sixty-second tale of gastric distress. "What quirks?" she asked, suddenly.

"I dunno. Can't think of any right off."

"'I didn't think so."

"You snort when you laugh."

"What?"

"You snort when you laugh. It's embarrassing." Charlie turned to his wife of seventeen long years. "Somebody tells a joke, and you either squeak or snort. I don't know why in hell you can't enjoy yourself like a normal person!"

Belinda pulled her pale housecoat tightly across her ribs. "Well, pardon me! They didn't cover laughing at finishing school."

"Finishing school... Ha!" he guffawed, and the evening battle began in earnest.

"I don't know what you're 'ha-ing' about, Charlie. At least I finished finishing school."

"What's that supposed to mean?"

"Nothing."

"You saying I'm dumb or something?"

"I'm not saying you're dumb."

"You saying I'm dumb, 'cause I was dumb enough to get married instead of gettin' my diploma?"

"I'm not saying anything. I'm watching TV."

"Well, you're right. I was dumb!"

Another commercial, although both had difficulty figuring what exactly the rapid-sequenced urban and pastoral scenes were supposed to be selling. Belinda turned to stare at Charlie's profile, aimed, lock-jawed at the television screen.

"It wasn't that dumb..." she mumbled.

"Maybe not," he still couldn't look at her. "But it would've been a hell of a lot smarter if I'd have waited."

If he had waited...

If she had not insisted on eloping that night...

If the young lovers they were back then could somehow have gotten an inkling of what they would become seventeen years later...

If only.

"I guess you'd probably be a doctor or something by now," Belinda mused. She smiled at the image of Charlie in his green scrubs, strutting through the emergency room like those handsome doctors on that Thursday night hospital show.

"What's so fancy about a doctor, anyway? So you get blood all over your pants, instead of grease. Is that so different?"

"It's easier to get out in the wash."

Belinda logic. Nothing set Charlie off quite like Belinda logic.

"Great. I'll become a doctor so you can have an easier time with the laundry!"

She recoiled from his anger. Sunk deeper into her corner of the couch. "At least it might make you more interesting, Charlie Caldwell."

"Whatta ya mean, interesting?"

"I don't know. More fun to talk to, I guess... More fun to show off."

"Hey. I'm sorry if I'm not entertaining enough for you! Sorry I embarrass you in front of your friends!"

"You don't embarrass me, Charlie. I didn't mean it nasty."

"Sure. Whatever."

A couple on the screen, unaware they were being observed, moaned in a passionate embrace, which made Charlie and Belinda increasingly uncomfortable. Charlie clicked the remote only to find another couple similarly occupied, so he pressed the channel button until he landed on a repeat of a World Wrestling Tag Team Match between costumed goons calling themselves the Chaos Brothers and the pairing of Grave Digger and The Zombie Man. Charlie raised the volume until their random grunts and body slams filled the conversational vacuum in the room. He settled back and unconsciously slapped his leg every time a wrestler crashed with exquisite choreography to the canvas.

Belinda hated wrestling, but not more than the dozens of other shows on this late at night. She imagined wrestling the remote from her husband's meaty paw, forcing him to talk to her; talk to her like married people were supposed to, like married people did on TV. But this wasn't TV. This was real-life and it was filled to bursting with ineloquent silences.

It had been years since they had any real conversations -- shared moments of discussion where issues were raised, debated and eventually resolved. Instead, their words, flung with hurt and sarcasm, hung in the air like a bad smell, then slowly dissipated, leaving behind feelings of embarrassment and offense.

"It's just..." the sudden intrusion of her voice in the room startled them both. "It's just I can't get you to talk to me about anything new and stimulating anymore. You know, like you used to."

"If you want new and stimulating, why don't you buy a damn computer. One of those that talk back to you." Click. Wrestling gave way to the non-stop excitement of televised fishing.

"At least it wouldn't be rude, Charlie Caldwell! You can't say two words to me anymore without one of them being rude!"

The large vein on his forehead began to throb again. "I don't have to take this, Belinda! I get enough frustration at the factory, without having to take this when I get home. All day long I get the whine of the screw machine in my ear. Then I have to come home and listen to you."

"Are you calling me a screw machine?" Tears immediately began to sparkle her eyes.

"No. I didn't mean..."

"You called me a screw machine! That's the nastiest thing I ever heard anybody call anybody!"

Although she was turned toward the TV, Charlie could see the hurt in his wife's expression. He hated to hurt her unintentionally. "Damn it all. I was just making a...whaddaya call 'em...an analogy!"

"You called me a screw machine..." Belinda whimpered. "That's not a nice thing to call somebody..."

"I didn't," Charlie muttered, in a tone others might have mistaken for defense or apology.

And so it went throughout the remainder of that show and the next. Complaint, criticism, insult and pain; an on-going lesson in marital non-dialogue, each unleashing verbal tirades about anything and everything, except what was really on their minds; like ignoring the poorly positioned coffee table that constantly outrages your shins, instead of moving it to the edges of the room, or better still, discarding it all together.

Closing credits scrolled over the unsteady trudge of a rowboat as it meandered its way toward shore and the scripted nirvana of a slow fade to black.

"So what's on tonight?" Belinda said finally, receiving no reply. "I said, what's on tonight?"

"I'm concentrating."

"What the hell are you concentrating on, Charlie? It's a deodorant commercial! There's only so much concentrating you can devote to deodorant."

His words took a long time unwinding themselves.

"Have you noticed the poetry has gone out of our marriage?" he asked softly.

"Poetry? Ha!" It was her turn to snort now. "All I remember was a lot of heavy breathing."

"Well...maybe my memory's better than yours."

She was surprised and chastened by the odd gentleness of his tone. "Okay...maybe there was a little poetry."

"A little," he sighed. "So what's on tonight?"

"I don't know," she paused, unsteady over this unfamiliar ground. "So where do you think it went, Charlie?"

"What went?"

"The poetry?"

It was too late. The mood had passed. Charlie reached for a box of KaBob's Pork Rinds and hollered, "Upstairs and first door on the left! Your mother locked it in her suitcase the day she unpacked the rest of her stuff!"

"Don't you go blaming my mother! If anyone had poetry, it was her and Daddy."

"Sure! That's 'cause he kicked off before the second verse. Anyone can have poetry if they don't have to hang around to listen to it."

"That's a cold thing to say, Charlie Caldwell. That was a cold thing to say."

"I didn't mean it to be all that cold..." Charlie felt their conversations were like Irish dancing on an ice-covered lake. "Look, I'm sorry."

"It's okay." Belinda paused, then said, "So what's on tonight?"

"I dunno. I didn't get a chance to pick up a TV Guide on the way home."

She nodded, and they each watched the channels screech by and meld in some chaotic montage far less distracting than the silence that weighed upon the room. Belinda looked at her husband, silhouetted in that eerie blue flicker, and wondered whether there was any place left for him in her heart.

They had been happy once, newlyweds eagerly devouring every moment spent together. But that was long ago, in lives that seemed to belong to other people, like remembering the back story of continuing sitcom characters. Belinda knew it was no longer about happiness, that elusive fiction foisted on the public by hack writers, and well-meaning therapists. Happiness was a lie, a construct, an advertising slogan sold to the public along with a deluge of appealing, but ineffective products. Buy this, they whispered. Buy this and you will be younger, more popular, more successful, less suicidal. She now knew happiness was simply the lure which seduced you into doing the right thing; a cold flame, captivating in its brightness, which eventually sputtered and died in the toxic atmosphere of personal responsibility. Their grandparents and their great-grandparents before them never spoke of happiness, or promised eternal bliss. Those were foreign words back then, in a language centered around obligation and duty. And so, in keeping with the family tradition, she daily pretended not to see the elephant of despair which occupied an ever-increasing corner of their lives, as if by ignoring the offensive creature, it might suddenly disappear and leave them the way they were so many years ago.

What was left bore little resemblance to the marriage they had once envisioned, had once boasted of to their friends, and had, for nearly two full years, actually enjoyed. Now they were merely playing house, with all the commitment of a children's game, but none of the joy. They climbed each day upon the moral rack, stretched between dreams of personal happiness and the burdens of family responsibilities. Another tragic landscape in the vast gallery of modern American marriage. Suddenly that thought was too much for her to bear, and she rose from the couch.

"You know, Charlie. This may sound crazy..." Her legs went weak and she turned away from his curious stare. "No. Forget it."

"Forget what?"

"Nothing. Never mind. You'd probably think I was crazy."

"I already think everything you say is crazy, so tell me."

She picked up the bag of pork rinds from the coffee table, clutched the cellophane encased treats tightly to her chest.

"I was just thinking...maybe it'd be fun if, you know, for a change...we shut off the TV and...you know..."

"And what? Finish your sentences, will ya? You snort when you laugh and you never finish your sentences!"

"Are you going to pick on me or listen?!"

"I'm listening. I'm listening and I'm not hearing. Maybe it's my ears, huh?"

"Maybe it is." She sighed as the words bubbled up from someplace long dormant. She pulled in a deep breath and said, "What I meant was...it might be fun to go parking in the car."

"Parking? We already got a driveway and a car port."

"No. I mean 'parking', Charlie. Parking. You know."

"Oh, parking! Like we used to."

"Yeah, like we used to, Charlie. The windows steaming up, and you grabbing me real tight and all."

"And you always getting your foot caught in the steering wheel. I never could figure out how you did that..."

She moved closer to him on the couch. "But it was fun, wasn't it, Charlie? We could lay right down on that front seat and see those stars right through the windshield. Way up there, twinkling bright as ever. Twinkling away like they were talking to us. Like they were telling us, it was okay what we were doing. Telling us they didn't mind..." She closed her eyes, and seduced him into her memory. "Those stars just winking and telling us that that's what they'd be doing, if they were our age and feeling like we did about each other."

She shook her head and smiled. "Lord, how I loved them stars."

"Yeah. The stars..."

"Remember, Charlie?"

"Yeah." He murmured, entranced.

"What do you remember, Charlie?"

His eyes fluttered shut, and he whispered, "I...I remember you...the way you were. Your blouse slipping off your shoulders...How they looked so soft and creamy warm with you lying there on the front seat. Just that little bit of light hitting you...That sure made me feel like something," he looked at her with a grin she hadn't seen in ages.

"You always did like my shoulders."

"Your shoulders? Hell, all of you. You were so...beautiful, Belinda. It used to make me so proud when you'd get all perfumed up and fancy looking just for me."

"Thanks, Charlie."

"It's true. You were so pretty, I'd get this tickly feeling right here in my ribs whenever I looked at you. The tickly feeling was so bad sometimes, I almost had to giggle. No other girl ever did that to me with just her eyes."

"Really?"

"Yeah." His voice throbbed with newly remembered excitement. "And remember the smell of my new Chevy? We'd get so close to the upholstery, you could smell that new car smell wrapping all around you. It was sorta like being right there in Detroit watching some factory worker stitch that seat up right before your eyes." He drifted back into the memory. "Man, that was something!"

"The stars...and the upholstery?"

He sighed. "Man, that was something."

They sat there as the memory embraced them, then slowly receded, taking their fading smiles with it. They each opened their eyes and were surprised to find the television still on.

After a moment, Belinda whispered, almost to herself. "The stars don't twinkle no more, do they, Charlie?"

"Naw... The stars don't twinkle no more." He ran a rough-knuckled hand through thinning hair. "And the upholstery hasn't smelled for years."

"Kinda sad, isn't it?"

"Kinda." He felt the pleasing look in her eyes resonate deep within his chest. "But hell, Belinda. We were kids then. Punk kids. We're all grown up now. You can't expect us to keep enjoying life like a couple of crazy kids."

"I guess not."

"I mean, where would we be today if we spent our lives acting like a couple of crazy kids? We wouldn't have the house. We wouldn't have the SUV. And we wouldn't have the kids."

"We'd have the kids," She giggled wickedly.

"Yeah. I guess we'd have the kids," He returned the smile. "But we wouldn't have the microwave, and we wouldn't have the big 4K TV."

"Guess not, Charlie."

She paused, as he dissolved from her eager lover of years past, back to the couch companion of the last seventeen years.

She could tell by his eyes, he saw the same sad transition in her.

"New TVs don't smell, do they, Charlie?"

"No. And they don't twinkle either."

They slowly turned their attention back to the flickering appliance, which beguiled them with game show beauty and sixty-second bursts of fulfillment.

To Belinda, it all felt so unbelievably sad.

Suddenly, she yanked the remote from his hand and clicked off the TV. He looked at her as if she had just varnished the baby.

"What do you say, Charlie? Let's take the car, and go out and find the stars? Okay?"

His shock slid into a tender smile. "Maybe steam up a window or two, huh?"

"Maybe," she dropped a tentative hand to his forearm, and lightly teased the dark, springy hair with her fingers. "What do you say, Charlie?"

His gaze moved from her eager smile to the tender hand on his arm. He desperately wanted it to be Belinda's hand, the old Belinda, but the touch gradually brought him back to this hand, this couch, their reality.

"Hell. Who are we kidding, Belinda?" he sighed. "We drive a Toyota now! Bucket seats. And besides, the weatherman said it's gonna be cloudy all night."

She returned her hand to the safety of her side. "All night, Charlie?"

"That's what he said."

"Well... Maybe the stars will be out tomorrow night."

"Maybe. He didn't give the long-range forecast."

"They never do," she said sadly, as she handed him back the remote control and slid back to her chosen corner of the couch.

"So, what's on TV tonight?" she sighed.

Slow Dance with a Stranger

"My mama always told me...she'd say, 'Pearl, don't you never go slow dancin' with a stranger.

Oh, you may think he's sweet and proper and oh too nice looking and all. But somewhere under that fine cotton shirt and smooth as honey smile is a heart tha's just waiting to pounce on a fresh young thing like you. And maybe you think it's okay because there are bundles of people around, and you like the music tha's playin' anyway, and you may as well.

But child, she told me, when he comes moving 'cross the floor like some fine looking stallion tha's suddenly found religion and wants to share it with you...you just pay him no never mind.

Slow dancin' with a stranger is the straightest path to a broken heart, and tha's the God's honest truth.

Now you think after hearin' all that, I'da listened to my Mama? Not me. I was sassy as a newborn goat. Always was. Always will be. Weren't nobody gonna tell me what to do...'specially when Mama ain't gonna be around to see!

So's on my sixteenth birthday, I throw on my prettiest blue cotton dress...comb my hair up all high and fancy, and walk my sweet young figure down past Main Street to the church social. Umm umm umm.

Then, I stand myself agin the wall for a long spell... 'cause the usual boys in these here parts are 'bout as plum ugly as a hog's brother-in-law...

Just when I start thinkin' about walkin' myself back home again, I feel this strong, smooth hand wrap around my fingers like a black satin glove made special for my little hand.

I look up...way up...and there stands the prettiest man the Good Lord ever seen fit to put on this here earth.

This man was tall and lean and smilin' away at me like he was the one that invented teeth.

I don't know who he is and nobody else don't neither. But the way he's tuggin' away at my arm, I know he wants to dance with me. This big, beautiful stranger wants to dance with me. Lord, what Mama would think to see us both together!

The first dance is a fast one, and I get all my giggles and nerves shook right outa me on that dance floor.

The second dance is even faster, but I'm really cooking now, and clapping my hands and kicking my legs like I don't care if there's nobody else on God's good earth but me and that big, beautiful stranger.

After a spell of spinning and laughing, the music dies away. I start to feelin' kinda shy and all, 'cause remember I'm just sixteen today and he's...well he's...he's every inch a man, from the bottom of his spit-polished leather shoes to the top of his twenny dollar hat.

So's I get real quiet, not wantin' to stare at him, 'cause I'm a good girl and I know what's respectable and what's not...but not wanting to take my eyes off him either, in case he ups and vanishes like a dream. He smiles that big grin of his, and I grin, too, and then he smiles so wide I'm half afraid his face is gonna split apart.

We both catch our breath and stand there, neither of us not ever wantin' to leave that dance floor. Then, he asks me my name in a voice smooth and soft as molasses, and I say "Pearl" right up and loud like I was queen of the county!

Well, that gets him to smilin' again, and without ever tellin' me his own name, he reaches up a strong, smooth hand and rests it on my cheek.

I don't even know this man's name, but he lays his big, gentle hand on my cheek like we was family. No. More than family...I swear, that man's hand on my cheek was like being kissed by an angel...

When the music starts up again, it's playin' real slow-like. I look up straight into that stranger's beautiful brown eyes and I just know I'm in a world of trouble.

With that slow, slinky music wrapping all around us, the stranger pulls me close to him, all gentle and firm-like, until my cheek is pressed right agin his starched white shirt. He smells so good, all of pride and respectability, and I know without even lookin' that every young girl on that dance floor was wishin' and hopin' it was them perched on his chest 'stead of me. But it ain't, and I'm the special one in that man's arms tonight.

That stranger moves me so smooth across the floor I swear my feet never touch no boards. When his arm curls back around me, I feel safe as a baby in her Mama's arms.

That is...until Mama showed up...

Next thing I know, I'm standin' all lonesome on the dance floor, and there's my little Mama whompin' the bejeezus outa that big, beautiful stranger. He's scurryin' around the dance floor, all curled up, trying to stop Mama's broom handle from messin' up his purty face. And he's screaming for her to stop and she's screamin' at him to keep his hands offa her little girl, and I'm screaming away 'cause I don't know what else to do. Everyone else is laughin' at the way me and Mama and the stranger is all carryin' on in the middle of a church social.

Finally, Mama's arm gets tired from whompin' on him, and the stranger sees his chance.

He high-tails it out the door, fast as a jackrabbit. Most people still say seeing that stranger fly outa that door with Mama and her wood broom right behind him was the high point of the evenin'.

When I got home, Mama whipped me good. Real good. I couldn't sit down without a cushion for three whole days.

So, my advice to you all is to never slow dance with a stranger.

'Cuz after not bein' able to sit my butt down for three days, I realize it just ain't worth it!"

Her Touch

"Some men, through their unwitting arrogance and tragic self-absorption, are destined to die alone. It was a bitter epiphany indeed, when he realized he was one of them."

Wallace Alexander Bonica stared at the words isolated on the wide-ruled notebook paper, stared at them for six full minutes, not blinking, hardly breathing. Stared at them so hard, his eyes reddened and then ached. The words struck a strangely responsive chord in him, which was only natural, since he had scribbled them down the night before.

Never a comfortable sleeper, Wallace had lapsed back into his frustratingly familiar ritual of abruptly waking at 3:02 AM for no discernible reason, other than it was suddenly 3:02 AM, and he had done so for as long as he could remember. He tried not to wake the beautiful raven-haired woman who slumbered peacefully beside him, and whose name he could not seem to recall. Autumn, was it? Or April? It was a calendar related name, of that he was sure.

As he rose, he was forced to remove a warm, delicate arm from across his chest, before he stumbled out of the large futon bed as quietly as he could without disturbing her enviable slumber. He gazed back at the sleeping figure, all grainy and shadowed in the semi-darkness, and noted how her long black hair spilled elegantly over his pillow, like hungry vines grasping for the next handhold up to the sunlight. He studied the gentle curve of her jaw, the soft sweeping line of her cheek, the tender slash of dark eyebrows, and realized she was beautiful. Painfully beautiful...and agonizingly young.

What was her name? January? June, probably. Yes, her name was June. He remembered now how she had offered to model for him in his studio, a young art student eager to be immortalized by the famed sculptor, Wallace Alexander Bonica.

Had she made love to him, or to his reputation? It hardly mattered, he mused, then suddenly grabbed the empty notebook and wrote two sentences, as if pushed by some unseen force.

"Some men, through their unwitting arrogance and tragic self-absorption, are destined to die alone. It was a bitter epiphany indeed, when he realized he was one of them."

He stared at those words now, and found it hard to imagine that they were his.

Wallace had never been an eloquent man, never saw the need to form sentences when a simple grunt or nod would do. For some reason, certain women considered this an attractive trait, as if he were hiding an ocean of raging emotion which only their love might be able to release. The truth was, of course, the opposite. There was never a raging ocean within him, not even a stumbling river.

He knew, to his own embarrassment, that inside he was as dry and empty as an abandoned well. Perhaps that was why he was so driven to be a sculptor, frantically seeking to uncover some meaning or depth in the withered husk of his soul, allowing the eloquence of his hands to communicate the screaming silence within, fashioning in clay or stone a beauty that his followers foolishly believed sprang from his essence, instead of his personal void.

The adulation had been immediate and unsatisfying. Groupies and sycophantic critics hovered around him since his first exhibit at age twenty. Now at forty-one, he had lost count of how many dollars he had accumulated, how many women he had made love to, how many works of art he had foisted on an easily deluded public.

That fragile patina of glory had worn rough in spots, and left him ever more uncomfortable with his art and his life. The adulation seemed hollow, a mocking echo of the emptiness within. He felt the barely noticed fleeing of years, and realized bitterly his life would only be measured in over-priced lumps of inanimate stone residue. Delicate, artistic tombstones, perhaps, but tombstones none the less.

And now, in the semi-darkness of his studio loft, Wallace Alexander Bonica dug his thirsty hands into a fresh mound of clay and tried desperately to feel something with life inside it.

****

He grew up in a broken family, of course, the quintessential breeding ground of lifelong insecurities and artistic passion. His mother was warm, loving and gone much too soon. His father never overcame the shock that his vibrant, affectionate wife would rather be loving random men in other states. He had married her for her seductive impulsiveness, somehow believing he could gradually wean her from the very trait that attracted her to him. Her steadfast determination to remain flighty and unpredictable caused the marriage to whither, and his father to retreat into a brittle shell of barely contained rage. As a discarded reminder of his wife's abandonment, Wallace became the target of his father's frigid indifference. Hugs were replaced by nods, conversations by notes stranded under refrigerator magnets. His father never remarried and Wallace never recovered. Yet, the rubble of his parent's marriage taught young Wallace a formative lesson about relationships.

It is far easier to leave a lover than to change her.

For the past three decades, he paid the terrible tuition for that lesson with a never-ending succession of encounters which could not even begin to penetrate his defensive ambivalence. Eventually, there was nothing left, except the facade and a nagging whisper of missed opportunity. Missed opportunity and the feeling that he was no longer quite real, that he was floating through the world like some emotional specter, barely tangible and never to be fully defined.

As he lay alone on the hard wood floor, staring up at the ceiling, his mind stormed through these thoughts and internal punishments. Daylight feebly attempted to push through his high loft windows, but was rebuffed by the dark curtains that were a gift from his mother when she had popped in unexpectedly one afternoon, before disappearing quite expectedly the same day. He tried to remember how long he had been lying on the floor like this, why the ceiling looked so fuzzy, and why he could no longer feel his fingers. A savage chill washed over him and rattled the moisture off his face. There can't be a chill, he thought, because it was mid-summer and he had repeatedly refused the plebeian comfort of air conditioning for his loft. As the room tumbled in downward spirals, he suddenly realized he must be sick. He tried to stand, but the bones in his legs seemed to melt under his weight, and he quickly crashed to the floor again.

Unable to move, with no one to call out to, he slowly began to comprehend the desperateness of his situation. He turned his throbbing head to scan the empty loft, and was sickened by its imposing sterility. Aside from the futon, a simple table and three mismatched chairs isolated in various corners, the massive room screamed of emptiness. No plants, no wall hangings, no telephone, no knick-knacks, no memories. The only items to distinguish his home from a prison cell were the four or five Wallace Alexander Bonica sculptures rising from simple wooden pedestals. Even viewed from this angle, with his throbbing cheek pressed against the unyielding floor, he knew they were beautiful; beautiful and tragic, the very words a former lover had once used to describe him as she walked out the door. He grasped desperately for her name, but it slipped away in a rage of fever and confusion.

A clammy sweat dripped into his eyes and mingled with tears. How strange the tears, he thought? He had refused to shed any since childhood. He didn't know why they plagued him now, and then suddenly, he did.

As he was swallowed by encroaching blackness, he knew he did not want to die here.

Not like this.

Not alone.

****

His eyes fluttered open in the soft darkness. and it took him a few more dulled moments to realize it must be night again. His artistry shimmered ghostly gray in the shadowy room; no longer beautiful, only tragic. He felt as if he could move now, and tried to claw his way to a standing position, but the dizziness slapped him down again. Slowly, painfully, he managed to crawl his way to the door. Knees scraping with agony. He groped for the door, but it seemed so very far away, a distant barrier to the outside world, like a promise never meant to be fulfilled. Yet, he sensed he would die if he didn't get help soon. With all his strength, he stretched for the knob, turned it, and stumbled into the corridor.

It took him another twenty minutes to make his way down to the street, and onto the front steps of his building, where his body was wracked by dry heaves. The emptiness inside screaming to get out. Though nothing emerged, spasm after fierce spasm, he seemed strengthened by the attempt. He dragged an arm across his damp, hair-streaked face and trudged stiffly to the subway entrance. People passed by as if he were invisible, or so uncomfortably visible in his wretchedness that they simply chose not to see.

Nothing seemed to be connected. He didn't move from one space to another, or even one moment to the next, but merely appeared, unable to remember where he had been moments before, or where he was headed. He moved through a blur of colors and harsh sounds, then found himself standing before a rush of subway trains. As if on cue, one screeched to a stop by his feet, disgorged its human contents and waited expectantly for him to enter its metal confines.

He could not.

He stared at the open doors, until they quietly retreated and the train fled down the darkened tunnel. Leaving him alone, the crush of humanity having left him abandoned and gasping in its determined wake.

The throbbing in his head had subsided with the cacophonous rhythm of the receding crowd. He was gravely ill, but in the concrete embrace of the subway station he no longer felt he was dying. Yet, he was ambivalent over his temporary reprieve. The sight of the subway tracks broke through his cloudy thoughts, held him fixed with the seductive promise of oblivion and release. They called to him with simple promises; no more feelings of disappointment and inadequacy, no more false praise or unrealized potential.

No more emptiness.

He took a short staggering step toward the edge of the subway platform.

Then another.

Then before his feet could move another step, a hand touched his forearm and changed his life forever.

Through dazed eyes, he looked down at the restraining hand, burning coolly against his fevered skin. A woman's hand, white as marble against his own olive wrist. A firm grip of support, not hesitant, not sexual, not even familiar. Yet, her touch seemed to pass right through his arm and grip him to his soul. His eyes wandered up the length of the arm to a woman's face, and he felt dizzy under her quizzical stare. The same white skin, sculpted gently around curious eyes, startling in their capacity to see right through him. Her lips were moist and generous, but held tightly by some unspoken inner turmoil. Never removing her hand from his arm, she studied his face intently, searching deep within him, for what he did not know. Then slowly, her eyes softened in obvious disappointment, and the smile that crinkled her lips was tinged with sadness.

"That's not the way home," she whispered, her voice a warm caress. "That's not the way. Believe me."

She would not remove her hand, as she had led him away from the lure of the subway tracks to the safety of the staircase. He let her lead him like a child out of the subway station up to the roaring street, and into the cool kiss of night air. He could think of nothing to say to her, except that he never wanted her to let go of his arm. When she did let go to flag down a taxi, he felt a piece of himself was suddenly ripped from his life. As she spoke to the cab driver something about a hospital, he noticed the subtle shimmer of her shoulder-length auburn hair under the street lights. The long, graceful curve of her neck and the elegant way her body moved without pretension or fear. He thought she was the most beautiful woman he had ever seen, but knew she wasn't. Yet, she had touched him straight to his soul, yet he was mystified as to how or why.

She came back to him, opened the rear passenger side door of the taxi, and gently pushed him inside. He watched in confusion, as she handed the burly driver a crumpled fifty dollar bill. Then she turned to him again with those eyes, those painfully expressive eyes.

"You have a fever. Feels like a bad one. The cab will drive you to the hospital. They will take care of you there."

He moved his mouth to speak. He wanted to know who she was. To beg her not to leave him. But the dizziness returned and no words would come out.

She seemed to understand. Her hand brushed the sweat-soaked hair from his forehead, then rested on his cheek with a soft caress. Her fingers like cool liquid on his face.

She searched his eyes once more, and again he felt he had somehow disappointed her. Despite his failings, she smiled reassuringly.

"I'm sorry," she murmured inexplicably, before the auburn-haired woman lightly kissed his damp forehead, closed the cab door and watched as the taxi pulled away into the night time traffic.

He watched her watching him, until she dissolved into an indistinct blur in a distant river of movement and sound. Then he closed his eyes and saw her face even more clearly, the way she searched his very core with her eyes, the way she resurrected his soul with one simple touch.

He would find her. He knew he could never again rest until the day he could lose himself in her eyes, in her touch.

As Wallace Alexander Bonica sunk back in the taxi on the way to the county hospital, he tried one more time to feel the strange woman's touch on his arm, and instead, finally found something inside himself he could believe in.

WHILE HE SLEEPS

For more than an hour, she sat up in bed and watched him snore beside her. The old grandfather clock downstairs told her it was now three o'clock, but she ignored its somber, reverberating tones.

She was concentrating.

Concentrating on his look. His sounds. His motions.

Even in the darkness, the shadows seemed to swarm around his thin, unshaven face. She watched his slack jaw fall open, as he turned with a bounce of the mattress, before burying the left side of his face in the soft feather pillow. He let out a fitful gasp, a soft moan, then silence.

She watched a trace of moisture form at the corner of his mouth, escape, and merge with the fabric of the pillowcase. She watched his nostrils flare, as his soft snoring again filled the darkened corners of the room.

She watched.

She studied his tumble of black hair, as it crawled across the pillow. The darting flutter behind the flesh curtain of his eyelids, his subconscious chasing dream images she dared not imagine. She followed the curve of his throat, the pronounced cartilage that swayed with every breath. The hollow cheek filled by sullen whiskers. The thick eyebrows. The thin slope of his nose, that in an earlier century might have been considered aristocratic. His lips, purple-black in the early morning gloom.

She could still smell the stale whisky on his breath, a sweet odor turning increasingly foul as the hours dragged on.

He slept on, oblivious to her stare.

Her face stung with a bruise which had not hurt for hours. Her arms folded protectively over the damaged ribs, which continued to ache with every breath. Her tongue traced the swelling of her lower lip, the taste of dried blood and bitterness.

He slept, and she watched him.

In the early morning gloom, everything about him repulsed her. She hated the way he made small clicking noises when he snored. Once it had amused, now it only disgusted her. She hated the sinister curl of his lips, even in slumber. And she despised herself for sharing his bed.

Suddenly he turned, rolled onto his back, as her heart leapt in her throat. What would he think if he woke to see her watching...staring...hating? Would he shout venomous words of contempt, the bile of a decaying marriage? Would he hit her repeatedly? Would her battered pride again keep her scorching tears to herself, until he was once more asleep? Was there room left in her tired, frightened body for any more pain and emptiness?

But he did not waken.

He remained asleep.

And her eyes could not let him go.

She thought of her son. The bruises and the excuses. His heart beating a dance of fear in his little chest, as she pulled him to a safety that was only temporary, only physical. An elusive haven in a continuing storm. Then a stinging backhand, and even that haven had vanished.

She knew it was the whisky. The frustrations. The pressure at work. Yet, the reasons were not enough to push back the savage contempt that welled up inside her as she watched him sleep.

She examined the sharp silhouette beside her. Traced the shallow creases caused by wrinkles in the pillowcase. She studied the contours of his face, desperately searching for something in them that she still loved.

But she found nothing, only rough whiskers and the promise of more violence.

She moved her hand a quarter inch above his face. His eyes did not open. She pulled it back, and continued to watch him as the old grandfather clock chimed four.

Another loud gasp interrupted his snoring, then receded like a fitful tide. He jerked his arm involuntarily, pulled along by some nightmare that would leave no bruises or scars when he awoke.

As she watched him sleep, she thought of her own dreams, her son's tears, the jagged shards of her life. Without looking, her fingers found the sharp embroidery shears she kept by her needlepoint on the nightstand.

She felt the comfort of the cold, unyielding metal, saw the glint even in the stifling darkness of the bedroom.

As he slept, she raised the deadly shears above his face. He shuddered, never knowing the peril which hung mere inches from his throat.

She prayed for the strength to end his nightmare...and her own.

Her hand trembled.

Then fell.

The shears returned to the safety of the nightstand.

Maybe tomorrow night.

While he sleeps...

DAWN'S COMING

"Dawn's comin'."

Wayne Packhammer rotated his heavy-lidded eyes to the purple-black, pre-dawn haze which settled over the wide expanse of Georgia farmland that had been his family's stomping ground for longer than he could remember. He dragged a worn flannel sleeve across the thin film of morning sludge encrusted on the corner of his mouth, then turned to answer his son.

"Yup," Wayne said with a nod.

He looked at his son now, silhouetted by the first itchy fingers of sunlight clawing their way up into the retreating night sky. Earl was nigh-on sixteen, with a gangly smattering of arms and legs too long for his slightly stooped frame. The boy had a long, thin nose and sharp features, in direct contrast to his father's round face and tree-stump bulkiness. Earl peered into the diminishing darkness with nervous jerks of his small head, furtive movements that brought to mind the skittish rooster, who continuously circled the barn opening, but almost never ventured outside.

Yup, concluded Wayne, that young'un was growing to be a fine strapling of a man, if Wayne thought so himself; though he would never admit such a prideful thing directly to his son.

Instead, he muttered, "Reckon it won't be long now, boy."

"You think?"

"Yup," pronounced the old farmer gravely. He took a hefty swig from a jug of corn squeezing,' and after a hesitation, passed it to the nervous teenager. "Figure they'll move in at first light."

Earl accepted the jug gratefully, took a quick gulp, grimaced at the powerful moonshine liquor, which burned a line of courage down his chest, as he coughed three times.

"Paw... Don't mind my asking this, but... "

"Speak your piece, boy. "

"Uh, cain't...cain't we get in real trouble for this?" stammered the boy.

He handed the handmade jug back to Wayne, who took one more swig, then placed the large crock behind the hay bale barricade for safety. Wayne considered his son's question for a long moment, as was his nature, then said, "All depends on what you mean by 'trouble.'"

"I mean, we might get ourselves killed and all. "

"If you're killed, you ain't got no more troubles. "

"I suppose not... But what if we just get all shot up and wounded like? "

Again, Wayne deliberated, his hand rubbing the rough stubble of his chin.   "That'd be trouble," he said finally.

A shadow, dark and indistinct, sailed up to their feet and flitted off. The two looked up to see a large hawk rise toward the morning sun, then gliding and hovering like a dream released.

Earl's fingers unconsciously moved up and down the stock of his old hunting rifle. "Or what if we kill a few of them and they lock us up for the rest of our lives?"

"That'd be trouble, too."

Another cough. Then Earl whispered, "So what're we doin' this for, paw?"

Wayne Packhammer pressed his thick lips together and checked the barrel of his rifle for the twentieth time that morning. "It's the principle of the thing, boy."

"Oh." Earl nodded, then used his binoculars to scan the small dirt road off in the distance. Nothing yet. He lowered the binoculars, and turned back to the burly old man plunked down on the hay bale like some Early American Buddha.

"Principle of what thing, paw?"

The Buddha rose with sudden vengeance, turning to his son with meaty hands clenched white on his rifle. "I'm not letting them take my land, boy! They're gonna have to drag me off it feet first!"

"But ain't there some other way?"

Again the big man studied the boy. Wayne would never have dared question his old daddy like this when the old codger had made up his mind to do something. Wayne tilted his head back and squinted at his son.

"You scared, Earl?"

"Hell, yeah!" squealed the young farmer, who became even more squeamish under his paw's dark appraisal. "You know I ain't never killed anything bigger'n a pig before. And that was only so's we could have him for Christmas dinner!"

"Well, these bank people are a darn sight bigger'n any pig."

"I imagine so." Earl replied softly. Suddenly, he looked to his father with wild, desperate eyes. "You don't think they'd send Charlie Waddell, do ya? His momma would sure be mad at me if I killed old Charlie."

Wayne grunted and slammed his rifle butt on the ground twice. "Charlie oughta know better'n to come and take my land. If he don't, then he's no better'n those Yankee bankers he works for." He laid the hunting rifle aside, turned and picked up the double-barreled shotgun, which leaned against the hay bale. His daddy's gun. "Besides. It just don't seem right for a man to work all day playin' with other folks' money."

"Whatta ya mean, paw?"

"Bankin'. It don't seem right somehow." A tone of wonderment crept into his gravelly voice. "I mean, they take all our money. Lock it up in that big old steel safe. Then they just sit there all day...watching that old safe, like somethin' magical's supposed to happen. Do it for weeks. Then, when I come to get my money back, they open up that big steel door again, take out my money...plus a little more that got 'interested' in it while it was just layin' there in the safe. And they give it all back to me, grinning like fools and sayin,' "Have a nice day, Mister Packhammer!" The old farmer slunk heavily down on the hay bale. "'Course I'm gonna have a nice day! They done gave me back my money, didn't they?"

"Seems kinda silly when you put it like that, paw."

"Don't seem natural. Like that three-legged calf that was born last winter." He shook his head, as if trying to decipher quantum mechanics written in Egyptian hieroglyphics. "Bankin's a lot like that three-legged calf."

The boy nodded. If a man as all-fired smart as his paw couldn't understand the complexities of the American banking system, how could Earl have a prayer of comprehending the situation they found themselves in now. With a nervous twitch of his head, he checked his gunsights by aiming his rifle at the ribbon of gravel road across the field. The very road the bankers would be coming down to take his daddy's land.

Earl shivered and spun his eyes back to the sky, which had melted to a watery blue-purple tint.

"Dawn's comin'," he whispered.

"Yup."

Alone in the field, they settled into an anxious silence together; each considering all the things which should rightly be said at a time like this; each finding it far easier to consider those things than actually express them. More darkness fled from the sky before Wayne mumbled, "Sorry I got you into this, boy."

"That's okay, paw. We all gotta die sometimes."

"That's sure enough true."

Earl kicked at a clod of stubble grass with the toe of his boot. "'Though I was sorta hopin' I'd get a crack at Melinda May Tagget before my time was up...if y'know what I mean?"

Wayne smiled. "Melinda May's a purty one. No denying that," Suddenly his mood shifted with the spreading light. He spread his thick legs and bellowed at the frightened youth beside him. "You think I'm a fool for defending my land, boy?!"

Earl startled at the sudden accusation.

"No, paw. I never, ever thought you was a fool!" He knew better than to think such disparaging things about his paw, yet he couldn't help but add under his breath. "I was just sorta hopin' I'd have a chance at Melinda May is all."

"I'm doing this for you, boy!" Wayne barked.

"I know, paw."

"My daddy farmed this land. And his daddy before him! And his daddy before him had to shoot a whole passel of Indians for this here land!"

"I know, paw. I know."

"What would they all say if we just let some silly bank folk grab it away from us without a fight?"

"They probably wouldn't say nothin', paw," Earl turned away, pretended to examine his rifle barrel. "On account of them being dead and all." He was embarrassed by the tremor in his voice when he added, "Like we's gonna be..."

"Mebbe." The gruff old farmer looked to the distant road leading to his property, and then to the yellow-tinged sky, which he felt to be deceitfully cheerful. "Dawn's coming up real strong now, ain't it?"

"Sure is," Earl gulped.

Wayne spit a black wad of tobacco at a scruffy bush and imagined the stern look in his own daddy's eyes. "Damn it all, this farm's been in our family for generations!"

"That's what I can't quite figure out, paw," Earl chose his words as if they were lengths of barbed wire. "If this farm's been in our family for so many generations...how come we owe so much money on it?"

Wayne sighed, he had asked himself the same question too many times these past few months. "Well, you remember when land values got real high and all? We borrowed mortgage money from the bank to buy that real fancy, new plow and harvester machine."

"That sure was a pretty machine."

"Expensive, too. But it was worth it. The salesman said it was gonna make us much better farmers."

They both nodded, remembering how the sparkly yellow paint glistened in the morning sun.

Earl turned again to his father. "So how come we didn't get to be much better farmers, paw?"

"Damn machine broke."

"That's right. I forgot." Although his father sat solid as stone on that hay barricade, Earl could not control his pacing. He forced himself to look off to the west acres, then asked over his shoulder, "Can I tell you something, paw?"

"I s'pose."

"Something real personal like?"

"You got something to say, now's the time to say it!"

The boy's words were barely audible.

"I hate farming, paw."

By contrast to his son's frozen stance, Wayne shot off the hay bale like he was sitting on cactus and only just realized it. "What'd you say, Earl?!"

"I said, I really hate farming, paw. Always did."

"But you're a fifth-generation farmer, boy!"

"I know. That's what's so darn funny about it all. I can't even stand the smell of pigs. I mean they really *stink!*"

His grandfather would have shot the boy down then and there, and considered it a good lesson in manners. His old daddy would have beat him to within an inch of his life. Considering what was soon to be coming down the road at them, neither parenting method seemed to make much sense to Wayne at that moment. Instead, he cocked back his head, squinted his eyes, and once again, took the measure of his son. "How come you ain't never told me any of this before, Earl?" His tone less harsh than his forbears would have liked.

"Didn't seem to matter none then."

Earl held his breath and fidgeted under his father's long, brutal gaze. After a stretched minute or six, the old farmer shook his head and spit.

"Pigs do kinda stink, don't they, boy?"

"That they do, paw." Earl smiled in relief.

"I mean," Wayne indulged himself a growing belly laugh, "I mean...if people smelled that bad, we wouldn't have hardly nothing to do with them, now would we?"

"Not me. No way!" the boy chuckled gratefully.

At that moment, the muffler-punctured rumble of an old Ford pick-up barked its way across the field. The growling sound froze the laughter within both their throats. Wayne quickly grabbed his binoculars and stared off across the field to the gravel road. In the new morning light, he could see the driver of the pick-up, as well as the three armed men in the sheriff's car behind him. "Looks like Charlie Waddell, and three, maybe four sheriff's deputies with him."

All the muscles tightened in Earl's thin face. "I guess this is it then, huh, paw?"

"Looks like it..." Wayne nodded solemnly.

Both men checked their guns one last time.

Wayne handed Earl an extra two boxes of ammunition, as each took ready positions behind the thick stacks of baled hay. Together, they raised their high-powered rifles and took aim at the approaching vehicles. Through their hunting scopes, they could clearly see the nervous faces of the lawmen as they scanned the too-quiet farmland.

"Paw?" Earl whispered, as both the pick-up and the sheriff's car rounded the curve at the entrance to the Packhammer property.

"Yeah, son?"

"You gonna shoot old Charlie, or you want me to?"

Wayne pressed his right cheek against his gunsight and slipped his finger into place on the cold, metal trigger. Out of the corner of his eye, he could see Earl bite his lip as he aimed his gun at his best friend's skull.

The invading vehicles moved closer. Wayne Packhammer steeled his jaw, and took one last look at his son, ready to carry on the family tradition. Then, with the delicious sarcasm of Nature, Earl's face was suddenly gold-lit by the rising sun, in such a way that the boy appeared to be kissed by dawn itself.

The silent war within Wayne Packhammer lasted only a few more seconds before he lowered his gun and sighed deeply. He placed his hand on the barrel of his son's rifle and pointed it toward the very ground his family had farmed for generations.

"Earl..." he said gently. "How's about instead of shooting old Charlie, you go out to the sty and shoot us a pig."

Earl's eyes widened in surprise and relief. "You serious?"

"That big, ornery one...and then we'll invite Charlie and those boys over for a big old ham breakfast."

"But what about the farm, paw?"

"Earl?"

"Yes, paw?"

Wayne leaned his rifle against the hay barricade. "I ever tell you how much I hate farmin'?"

"Go on! You?!"

The old farmer scratched the whiskers on his chin with a soil-smudged hand. "Never seemed quite natural for a man to play in dirt and pig shit for a livin'." He picked up his double-barreled shotgun and carefully ejected each deadly cartridge. "Sort of ironic, don't ya think?"

"No, sir!" The boy tossed his rifle to the ground and gazelle-leaped straight into the air. "Does this mean I get a chance with Melinda May Tagget?" he shouted.

"Might as well." For the first time in more than ten years, Wayne Packhammer threw a big old arm around his son's shoulder. "And mebbe

I'll try my hand at banking," he added with a sniff of the air. "Banking...yep, I could grow to like that."

"Maybe you could ask Charlie for a job, paw?"

"Mebbe..." considered the big man, as he led his boy back to what would be the family farmhouse for only a few more hours.

MOM'S BAD DAYS

"I don't know why everybody makes such a big fuss about it. It's not so bad, once you get used to it.

I remember I used to get really scared at first. All that screaming. The crying. The way she gritted her teeth when it happened. That was the scariest part of all...You could always dodge the fancy china when it splattered against the wall and flew apart like a dozen little white butterflies. And those straw baskets with the dried flowers never really hurt, even when they hit you smack in the face. And now that I think about it, it didn't really take all that long to pick up everything after it was all over.

But the worst part...the part I could never forget...was her teeth. Yeah, her teeth. I still see them at night sometimes. The way they would just clamp together real tight, like a hard, white wall trapping the Mom I used to know inside. Those teeth would press so tight together, she couldn't ever get out, even if she tried to. Then her lips would snarl up and curl way back, almost like they were as scared of her teeth as I was.

Daddy would try to rush all us kids out of the room, and pretend like we didn't see any of it. Like it never really happened.

And he'd always have that same funny look on his face. His eyebrows would go way up on his head and his top lip would pull down and twitch a little. I think if Judy or Cathy or I ever said a word to him, when his face was like that, he would've just fell right over and cried. I bet he would have.

He'd always say he loved us very much, then rush us into bed, no matter what time it was. Then he'd go back in the kitchen and try to wrestle Mom down until those teeth freed her, and she stopped screaming and she became Mom again.

As for me, I'd lie in bed listening to the dishes breaking, and try to dream of little white butterflies flying off to somewhere safe. Somewhere quiet.

Somewhere this wouldn't ever happen to kids like me."

ELEANOR BOYLE

Eleanor Boyle worked the cotton candy machine at the Iowa State Fair, which was, surprisingly, not as fulfilling a career as you might think.

When she was a wide-eyed, pudgy child of seven, working the cotton candy machine at the Iowa State Fair seemed like the most perfect job in the whole world. You got to be part of that magical moment when sugar transformed itself into lacy, spidery strands of pure childhood joy. You would always have that pink, sticky smudge of melted sugar painting your fingertips, which was always great for running through your little brother's hair whenever he was being annoying, which was pretty much all the time. And most of all, you got to eat all of your mistakes.

If the angels had a job in heaven, seven year-old Eleanor thought, it must be making cotton candy into clouds.

Ever the headstrong little girl, Eleanor Boyle set out on the path to achieve her career objective. She started wearing too much make up, and hanging around the traveling fairs and festivals any chance she could. She found every reason to fight with her parents, so they wouldn't think twice about holding her back. Finally, on the summer of her seventeenth birthday, Eleanor Boyle slipped out of the house with her mother's cookie jar money and ran off to join the carnival, which was already packing up to go to the next State Fair in Missouri.

After four years of working ticket booths, corn dog stands and strawberry shaved ice counters, she finally graduated to the cotton candy machine, and had been happily spinning her wares ever since.

The carny life is an exciting one, filled with splashes of color and noise, distinctive smells and ten thousand new faces a night. No city ever got the chance to feel familiar, because you were always setting up, working long hours, packing, then moving by truck or rail to the next set up, hundreds of miles away. During the peak summer months came the elegant State Fairs – Illinois, Pennsylvania, and maybe even Connecticut, if you were lucky and the tour manager didn't cheat the previous year's venue operator.

The spring and fall brought the smaller festivals and neighborhood celebrations. The winter, a chance to rest your feet in Florida for a few precious weeks, before the carny cycle would start all over again.

Eleanor was proud of the fact that she had spun her cotton candy in twenty-seven separate states. She had the soul of an artist, and wielded the paper cones like magic wands. Eleanor Boyle -- The Cotton Candy Queen, they called her, because no one could spin as fine a tasty silk as she could. State after state, year after year, season after season, she laughed and spun her sugary sweet webs for the best and worst of humanity. And she pitied the poor souls who could only visit a carnival once or twice a year.

Yet, as she approached her fifty-third birthday, Eleanor felt something was missing in her life. It wasn't sex, you could always find plenty of that behind the Tilt-A-Whirl with any number of leather-skinned carny boys. They were all over-tanned, slightly grimy, and usually had more tattoos than teeth, but they were always willing to give her a free ride.

No, it was something else.

It wasn't love exactly, because she found that in the adoring eyes of the ravenous little children as she handed them huge gobs of her colorful concoction piled high and sticky on white paper cones.

It wasn't even intellectual stimulation, for the last thirty-two years she had been attempting to comprehend the physics that turned solid sugar into spidery strands of sweetness. Maybe it was just that same aspect of physics; her once solid life seemed no more than wispy filaments; always alluring, but increasingly insubstantial.

As she perched on a barstool in the traveling fair's last night in Boise, she sipped her beer and sucked on one of her omnipresent cigarettes. Never one to be swept away by philosophical musings, Eleanor wondered to herself what had suddenly made her feel so dissatisfied with her chosen career.

It wasn't hard to figure out. It was him. The man who bought $13.95 worth of pink and blue cotton candy this past shift. He was the most beautiful man she had ever seen...tall, with eyes as blue as the Scrambler seats, and a gentle smile that made her heart soar like the Ferris wheel. He had a head of tussled blonde hair that gave him a little boy charm, unlike the rough thin men of the carny circuit, who always maintained the appearance of old beef jerky. The $13.95 man had a small girl perched on his shoulders, and two slightly older boys tugging at his sleeves. His square-jawed face bore the happy exasperation of all fathers trying to reign in their children at this sprawling ride, game and sugar complex designed to send those same kids bouncing through the midway like radioactive popcorn. It was an expression she had seen daily in her decades as Cotton Candy Queen. But what made this scene different, what tugged at her heart was the adoring expression on the face of the woman snuggled comfortably under the $13.95 man's free arm. A woman happy with the world, because she was loved by this beautiful man and his frantic children. The woman even looked a little like Eleanor, except maybe a little younger, a lot thinner, much prettier and without a mouthful of teeth yellow-browned from a three-and-a-half pack-a-day nicotine habit. Still, as Eleanor Boyle handed the blonde man his generously apportioned cones, she could almost picture herself on the other side of the counter, snuggled comfortably under his arm, smiling contentedly into those deep, Scrambler-seat blue eyes of his.

The man made sure each of the children said 'Thank you, Ma'am" to Eleanor after receiving their cotton candy. Eleanor even tried to give him a free bag of sweetness for himself, yet he refused with a polite grin.

"Wouldn't be right, Ma'am," he said with a voice more enticing than any carnival barker. "That would be like taking money that rightly belongs to your employer. And that just wouldn't be fair."

Of course, she fell in love with him at that exact moment. The concept of being fair with other people's money was not a commonly heard theme in a carnival midway. Spike, the three-balls-for-five-dollars man, hardly worried that the desperate fathers and pride-pumped boyfriends had virtually no chance of knocking over the lead-weighted milk bottles in his booth. Marnie, the two-darts-for-a-dollar girl felt no remorse that even the occasional marksman would only win a prize worth less than a nickel, which he could eventually trade up to a larger stuffed animal after only six more bulls-eyes and an average investment of thirty-eight to forty-four dollars. And Boris, wasn't too worried about being fair with other people's money, either.

Boris sat behind one of the few remaining exhibits tied to the original freak show days from which all carnivals evolved, but which human rights and political correctness had all but eliminated.

Boris ran 'The Amazing Woman With The Body Of A Snake' trailer in the back of the midway. Of course, The Amazing Woman With The Body

Of A Snake was only a mannequin's head glued to a six-foot rubber tube, but people didn't realize that until they spent $3.50 worth of ride tickets to inspect it up close. Then they would feign this amazed look, so no one would realize they had gotten conned out of three-fifty by such an obvious hoax. In fact, they would leave the trailer looking so astounded, other people passing by would rush in to pay their money to see the dummy head and rubber tube, in what eventually became an unstoppable chain reaction of embarrassed suckers.

Now, as Eleanor Boyle sat in the smoky bar on closing night, she realized that what she needed was someone who appreciated her outside of her cotton candy stand. For thirty-six years, a rotating swamp of carny boys had been her only family. She had, in turn been their part-time mother, occasional lover, and frequent drinking buddy. But this sense of belonging was as impermanent as all the cities and states they passed through each season, like empty soda cans crumpled and discarded on the road. Each one of them knowing the carnival life was no place to build a family.

As she filled her mouth with the bitter sharpness of her fourth draft beer, Eleanor Boyle knew her reign as Cotton Candy Queen was coming to an end. It was the only job she had ever known, and at fifty-three, the idea of taking on a new life in the outside world, away from the smoky comfort and noisy familiarity of the midway seemed intimidating. Still, she had her little 'set-aside' money, and that would help.

Since she was seventeen, Eleanor Boyle had set-aside a few pennies or dollars out of every paycheck, for the inevitable day she would become too old, or too broken down for the carny lifestyle. She bought stocks two or three shares at a time, mostly based on things she saw on the midway, or conversation fragments that rose above the symphonic roar of a thousand visitors and day. Over the last few years, words like Facebook and Google flittered above the music and laughter. Knock-off Disney characters, changed just enough to avoid copyright infringement, a brightly painted Apple in the hands of an old hag, or a proud Amazon with spear held high. She'd scribble down the words, then check the Finance section of the local paper to see if any of them matched. Whenever she found a Disney, an Apple, an Amazon or a Facebook, she'd plunk down her crumpled bills at the nearest discount broker and hold on to them with fierce loyalty. By fifty-three, those few dollars each week had accumulated into a respectable nest egg in her self-managed portfolio. She did the math in her head and estimated her set-aside money at around one million, nine-hundred and seventy-three thousand, four hundred and twelve dollars...based on today's closing prices on Wall Street. Not exactly where she planned to be at fifty-three, but it'd do. She had anticipated two million-three by this point in her life. She would have made it, too, if she hadn't listened to Clive at the fun house, who told her to dump her Microsoft and Intel stock and buy Digital, because the Alpha chip was going to run Pentium II sales into the ground.

Clive was good at scaring little kids, but he didn't know shit about the technology sector.

By the time she had swallowed the last bubbles of foam from the bottom of her glass, Eleanor Boyle had made her decision. One million, nine-hundred and seventy-three thousand, four hundred and twelve dollars would be enough to live on while she went to cosmetology school, or became acquainted with the hamburger trade. It may not be as glamorous as cotton candy, but sometimes life required changes and sacrifice.

As Eleanor pushed away her barstool, she nodded to the carny boys drinking down the day's last solace. They recognized that look in her eye. It was the look all travelers get when they suddenly realized they've spent too much time on the road. She slowly nodded to Clive, to Randy, to Boris, Spike and Marie.

"I've spun my last cone, boys," she announced with a twinge of regret and defiance. They each nodded silently in return.

Then Eleanor Boyle, the Cotton Candy Queen of twenty-seven states, walked determinedly out into the cool night air, in search of a handsome arm she could fit comfortably underneath.

FIRST NIGHT

The room reeked of her, though she had never once set foot inside it. No, she wouldn't be caught dead in a place like this. Yet, hidden in every corner cringed an argument too bitterly fought. In every shadow lurked an accusation too ugly to be true. In every framed painting grew not a peaceful pastoral, but a slow filleting of the soul, as if the tranquil scene of generic barns was designed to mock the raging chaos in his life.

He was lord of no more than this domain. A $39 a night efficiency room, seven and three-eighths miles away from where this night should have ended, had he not been selfishness incarnate. Or worse, detached to the point of non-existence.

His eyes scraped the walls, the ceiling, the TV, hungry for distraction, but the twenty-four hour news anchor, with her pitifully perfect hair and empty smile, seemed to speak not of stock prices, but of guilt and disappointment, as if even today's weakening of the market had been his fault.

All his fault.

An 'efficiency unit' they called it, but there was little that was efficient in this ill-fitting room, overrun with hastily plundered belongings. Piles of clothes shoved in black plastic garbage bags huddled in the corner, some he had not worn in years, but grabbed anyway, because they were his and he so desperately needed to take what was his from a home that soon would no longer be. As if removing the evidence that he had ever been in that place might also remove the shame of his inadequacies as a husband, as a provider, as a human being.

A better man could have made it work. A patient man. An understanding man.

But in the screaming rush to grab what was his, he had forgotten to take with him even a fragment of understanding. And the near-empty bottle of aged bourbon in his hand provided no further insight, just a blessed dulling of the confusion.

Lying on his back, head propped at an uncomfortable angle by two stiffened motel pillows, plus one he rescued from his own bed just hours before, he slowly took inventory of the personal pillaging of his marriage. Random paperwork, one pair of shoes, too much underwear and not a single sock. The computer, of course, for there was more of him in its electronic hallways than there was left in this aging body that had somehow shut down years ago, and numbed itself to life. He really didn't know why he had taken the rest: a chipped coffee cup with no special meaning or attachment; a box of Happy Meal toys he had one day meant to drop off at the local children's home; last year's tax receipts; and this year's scribblings of increasingly vacant thoughts and inspirations.

Fourteen pens…

One wok…

An old coat...

A broken umbrella...

And ten thousand and twelve half-felt memories.

Now as he lay, open-eyed, battling to sleep, a caustic chuckle struggled to steal out of the widening black hole in his chest, but couldn't. It just couldn't. He tried to amuse himself with the irony of how, in just a few hours, he had moved from a king-sized bed wide enough to share a twenty-year ravine with a woman who had once felt closer to him than his own skin, only to end up in this inappropriately named twin bed that barely had room for him alone.

Him alone.

So this is what separation feels like.

This is the place wounded marriages go to die.

He tried to catalogue his emotions, but none felt half as noble as he had hoped or expected. He had done nothing 'for the best.' Even as he began to build the defensive spin that he would tell so often that he might one day even believe it to be true, the smoke-stale air of the cheap motel room saw right through him.

This was it – his first glimpse into the terrifying tunnel of onrushing divorce.

No matter how high he cranked the frustratingly loud heating unit, he remained numbingly cold. Chilled, from the bloodstream out. It was a feeling he knew he would have to grow used to, with no warm, but resentful arms to hold him, spoon-like, as he began the long, first night struggle for sleep. No one to hear his moans or grudgingly wake him from the nightmares that had plagued him these last few years.

So this is what separation feels like.

With only three hours down, and a bleak four or five decades left to go.

ESCAPE

Even Bartley Farrow had to concede his life was damned impressive in its sheer and blinding normality. Two teenagers, Fred and Jane, who alternately tolerated and ignored the fatherly pronouncements he felt compelled to make; Dustball, a small gray wiener dog who year after year refused to be housebroken; and a downtown office job, which over a fourteen year, seven month period had sucked a little more of the spirit out of him each day, yet he could not muster enough will, annoyance, or ambition to walk away from it. To top it all off, there was Helena, a wife of nineteen years who despised him, because he had long ago ceased to be the man she somehow believed she had married, or would be able to sculpt into someone better.

As much as he hated to admit it, Bartley had long ago become unrecognizable even to himself. Perhaps he might have found consolation if his gradual erosion of identity was the result of some cataclysmic psychic overhaul, a long repressed memory of childhood terror, or a traumatic restructuring of his priorities. But it wasn't. He had simply and systematically given what he considered to be himself away in barely noticed increments, surrendering little bits of who he was, and what he cared about, with each passing moment.

Bartley Farrow had stepped dutifully into the quicksand of numbing routine, expecting to leave shallow footprints, yet realizing too late how much he had become too insubstantial even for that.

He allowed himself to be stripped to the bone in the modern marketplace of the middle-aged man. In exchange for security, he let go of both fear and desire. He paid for cheap stability with youth and idealism. Bartered love for acceptance. Purchased predictability by sacrificing his innermost dreams. And obtained sterile comfort at the price of passion.

No pound of flesh was required. The going price was his very soul.

How quickly it all had crept up and burrowed into him. Relationships vanished, as people were reduced to easily digested categories, never actually known. Trivial events now achieved ominous significance, while the important issues of his youth became too noisome to consider. His entire life seemed to slip into one amorphous, all-consuming generality. And even that was too tedious to consider.

Bartley Farrow could not pin-point when the change began. He never expected any of this to happen. One day he was the quintessential teenager, furiously frothing with defiance and blustery dreams. Then somehow, somewhere, somewhy, angry potential gave way to the rasping expectations of others, like a soft, unspoken whittling of his soul. With the blink of a hindsight eye, there were mortgage payments, dependents, responsibilities, community standing, and a billion other piranha-like worries. Too late, he recognized the terrible trap his father had fallen into, becoming so distracted by the myriad details of growing up, that he had allowed shadowy time to steal away his youth. On this Tuesday afternoon subway ride, Bartley Farrow suddenly found himself staring at his fellow passengers through an older man's eyes, dull, weak and bewildered.

The subway car lurched awkwardly, knocking him against a scowling white-haired grumble of a man, wrapped in a rumpled brown suit, clutching his tattered lather briefcase like it contained every memory he had ever made. They exchanged grimaces, each recognizing a fellow traveler on the road to weary irrelevance.

Bartley remembered how he had once smirked whenever his father still referred to those elderly acquaintances as "kids". Now it all seemed so unspeakably tragic. Years were never meant to go by so quickly. As the subway smoothed and rattled on, Bartley was overcome by a fierce, futile longing to escape to a place where nobody used expressions, like "What's gotten into you lately?" "You've never done that before." and "That's just not like you." These were words with chains, and he was already so weighted down by self-imposed restrictions, his chest began to ache.

His eyes wandered the subway car, hoping to find someone else to be. The loudly laughing street toughs. The bickering Asian couple, who at least still talked to each other in their angrily lilting Mandarin. The shaggy, sullen-eyed subway musician, caressing his guitar case, the only lover who truly understood his need to be.

Bartley longed to grow a beard again. Kiss a strange woman just to see how her lips tasted. Or suddenly drive to New Mexico, in search of some elusive wisdom or ancient magic he no longer believed in. He yearned for the freedom to be frivolous, to indulge reckless thoughts without immediately dismissing them as childhood fantasies.

He knew his children despised him for the shallowness he had years ago mocked in his own father. He saw it in each roll of their eyes. His wife performed her routine conjugal duties once a month, with just enough enthusiasm to keep him from straying. When not leaking his days away at the office, Bartley Farrow lost interest in any activity which forced him to step out his front door, much less past his driveway. He watched endless hours of situation comedies he detested. Watched without a twinkle of amusement. Watched because he called it 'relaxing.'

He had once dreamed of being a rock star, a famous scientist, a world-class painter, and a lover of many women. Now his grand ambitions had been systematically reduced, sterilized and shrink-wrapped; malleted into the stark right angles of suburban acceptability. They became shadow whims, distant as a stranger's whispered laments. Gone were the longings for fame and adoration. Now he dreamed only of a solitary subway seat, and being left alone in the evening to hide himself, without disturbance or judgement, in the sterile sitcoms he so desperately hated.

Little by little, everyone he knew fell out of his imagination. Bartley dreamed only of cocoons and armor.

Bartley Farrow recognized a gnawing blackness which threatened each hour to encroach onto his field of vision. It came in terrifying and irresistible waves when he was alone. He knew, if he wasn't careful, it would one day obliterate everything. He would lose himself, if he didn't continually force it back down into that insistent cavity hidden deep within his chest.

****

Friday. 10:45 PM.

Bartley sat in his worn easy chair not watching the show he always didn't watch at this hour. Fred and Jane were both out on dates with other posturing, arrogant teens he despised. Their appeal to his children was greatly enhanced by his very disapproval of them. Bartley ground his back molars in distaste. Fred and Jane were sure to ignore their curfews yet again, and he would do nothing about it, once again.

Helena claimed she was making crafts for the church bazaar, but was probably in the arms of that dark-haired college boy she had bumped into at the corner grocery store. Bartley envisioned how she was bumping into him now, and a bitter fluid rose in his throat.

Surrounded by the sounds and smells of a house grown suffocatingly familiar, Bartley sat alone in the semi-darkness with his bottle of Jim Beam. He felt his thoughts swirl and die in golden rivulets of bitterness and regret. He looked up to see Dustball pee on the rare oriental rug in the corner, the last remnant of a time when personal choices mattered. He took a heavy swallow, felt the irritating heat comfort his soul and senses, then channel-surfed as if his TV remote control was the magic wand which would at last help him find the peace and happiness he no longer believed was possible.

Peace and happiness. The deceptive twins of adulthood. The eternal marketing ploys which dragged you, uncomplaining, through a substandard life, and kept you frantically seeking a reward you knew would never be paid.

Peace and happiness.

He somehow felt he should have known better.

✳✳

The long, lonely minutes dropped off the clock like waves of drugged lemmings. Bartley stared at a brown paint splotch on the wall until it seemed to pulse, then disappear entirely. Dustball yapped and scampered by his feet, then looked up at him with eyes both pitiful and full of accusation. He threw a laconic kick at Dustball, and even though he missed, the dog slunk back to its spot on the oriental rug.

Forty-five minutes after her curfew, Jane walked in. She threw little more than a defiant nod at her rumpled father, before fleeing up the stairs to the sanctuary of her bedroom. Half an hour later, Fred repeated the ritual, only without the nod. It was nearly 2:00 AM when Helena stumbled through the door, eyes softened with guilt-induced affection. She walked over to Bartley and kissed the top of his head. As she stood behind him, she mumbled some half-hearted story about meeting her girlfriend in the grocery store and losing track of time, which she knew he wouldn't believe. Still, he was grateful that she at least felt obligated to spin the tale to its unenthusiastic conclusion. Bartley nodded at the appropriate points, and tried his best not to notice how substantially cleaner her hair was now, than when she had left. He tried desperately not to acknowledge the scent of an unfamiliar shampoo. When her story finally petered out, she kissed Bartley on the head a second time and retreated into the hallway.

Without looking at him, she climbed the stairs and asked, "Are you coming to bed?"

"In a few minutes," he replied, but she had already safely escaped behind the bedroom door with secret memories he could only envy her for having.

****

Bartley Farrow sat in the safety of his easy chair knowing he would eventually have to climb the stairs back to his chosen life. He knew he should scream. Perhaps even confront his wife in a fit of jealous rage. Yet, he also knew that once he saw her face on the pillow, her delicate features made painfully angelic by the soft application of sleep...a peaceful repose he hadn't shared in years...once he saw her hair spill across the pillow, her eyes flutter gently with dreams he was sure no longer included him, heard her soft lips part to softly exhale all her troubles; once he saw her like that, he knew he would forgive her. He hated himself for not having the strength to fight for her. For no longer loving such a sweet and lovely creature. For surely this affair must be his fault. Just like everything was his fault, an understandable consequence of detaching yourself from the world.

He realized then, that even numbness had its price.

Bartley watched the splotch on the wall again. He listened to the familiar chimes of the grandfather clock in the hallway, the rumpled creeks and complaints of the old house. He noticed another large puddle surrounding Dustball, who looked up at him, then flattened her ears back and bobbed her head with guilt and submission. It was at that exact instance, in the mocking comfort of his favorite chair, that it all became too much for Bartley Farrow. The wife...the job...the kids...they all stuck in his throat like a half-swallowed cocklebur that refused to budge.

Suddenly, the long-feared blackness rose up in him.

His knuckles whitening as he death-gripped the armrests.

His heart pounding in his eyeballs. A tingle of sweat escaping from his hairline.

He knew what he had to do.

****

With a swiftness he hadn't felt in years, Bartley Farrow dashed to the hall closet and grabbed his father's old duffel bag. He spilled its contents of discarded shoes and boots onto the floor with a loud 'kerbash,' then listened to hear if anyone responded.

They didn't.

He was as much a ghost to them as they were to him. He strode triumphantly back into the living room, reached down to grab the dog by the collar and shoved the unresisting animal into the duffel bag. Dustball was too surprised to yelp.

Bartley tied a large Boy Scout knot in the top of the duffel bag. He threw it over his shoulder, enjoying the shifting, squirming weight within. He shoved his feet into a pair of old leather workboots had once owned but never wore, grabbed the car keys and wallet from the top of the microwave oven, and walked out of the world he knew too well.

****

As he drove his battered minivan through the uncluttered and uncolored streets, Bartley was surprised at how sanitized everything looked in the harsh silver glow of a full moon. Through his tightly closed windows, the familiar houses looked like silent parodies of themselves. The lawns like great expanses of empty excuses. He suddenly felt very foolish. He had tossed an aging mutt with a bladder problem into his father's old duffel bag and somehow convinced himself it was an act of daring and independence. He prayed no one would see him, and as he prayed, someone did.

Her large eyes startled him and he stomped on the brakes instinctively. The screechy whine of the tires made him feel even more foolish. The old minivan limped and shrugged apologetically up to the young hitchhiker by the side of the road. To Bradley's horror, she mistook his panicked stop for an invitation. She picked up her neon green backpack with a half-trot. As she reached the decades old minivan, she peered in the passenger side window at the silent man with the vacant expression. She smiled and mouthed something he could not understand.

Bartley stared back at her through the closed window as if he were the lone occupant of a fishbowl.

She spoke again, but the words were muffled. He stared at her curiously, until he realized she was asking him to unlock the passenger's side door. Expecting him to admit her into this childish early morning tantrum. The color rose in his cheeks, and he felt suddenly grateful for the emotion-hiding pallor of moonlight. He leaned over to open the door, wishing he were back home in his old recliner, watching his familiarly unfunny sitcoms.

The door opened.

The girl tossed the neon green backpack onto the floor and followed it with a leg too shapely to escape notice. He blushed further as she slid her youthful frame into the tattered bench seat beside him.

"Thanks," she gushed. "You're a lifesaver."

He drove off without asking where she was going. He drove off because driving was safer than talking to this beautiful woman-child with the long brown-blonde hair and the too-enticing smile. When she rolled down her window, the cool breeze caused her glistening hair to dance with abandon.

After a few minutes of heart pounding silence, she asked him his name. He told her with a tightly controlled voice, and she wrinkled her nose in amusement at the sound of it.

'Bartley Farrow' she mouthed silently with lips so young, so irreverent, so alive. It was slowly becoming the single most embarrassing and thrilling night of his life.

Without another word on his part, he learned her name was Angel. That she was a Philosophy major at Georgetown. That she had just last week received a ride from a rock group known as the Psychological Band-Aids, who drove her to Evansville in a beat up old van, and sang to her the entire way.

He did not ask what would possess her to hitchhike at three in the morning. She seemed to belong here. Belong to the night.

He drove and listened to her disjointed stories. She was only a few years older than his son, but he did not think of his family now. Could not. The road and her words seemed to unwind with the same comfortable pace. He knew he would never remember a single thing she was saying, but her voice and her conversation touched him in a way no one had for years. She talked to him, not knowing what he was like. Not caring what mistakes he had made in his life. Not judging him for his aloofness, or his pain.

She spoke to him, as if he was real.

And because of that, he felt years slip away with every turn of the odometer.

Bartley made a conscious effort to try not to stare at her, especially her legs. Or the small curves of her too-perfect breasts. Through an occasional sidelong glance, he realized she was beautiful. Painfully beautiful, like bright sunlight on moving waters. He detected a slight Asian tilt to her generous eyes. And an easy smile that tightened his stomach and made him feel like giggling.

She noticed his attempts not to notice her, and was amused by them. Her laughter was liquid sunshine. He felt safe with her. But there was something more. Without threat or request, she had insinuated herself into his world.

'This was what it was like to be alive,' he thought. He realized how easy it would be to lose himself in her gentle, laughing eyes.

"What's in the duffel bag?" she asked with a glance towards the back seat, and Bartley felt the words like an icy slap to the face. His forehead broke out in a cold sweat. Perhaps she was with the Humane Society and he would be arrested. Or worse, she would think he was some kind of psychopath and leave his car...and his life...forever.

"Uh...my laundry," he said, with a conviction that would have fooled no one.

"Your laundry?" she repeated softly.

"Yes. I'm taking my laundry to the...uh...the laundry."

"Uh huh."

"It's perfectly natural. Lots of people have dirty laundry," he mumbled, and if he could have slapped his own face without appearing even more ridiculous, he would have.

"Well, Bartley Farrow, midnight rescuer of stranded ladies…" she said as she leaned over agonizingly close to his ear. He could feel her warm breath play delight on his skin. His pulse quickened as her hand rested upon his shoulder. "Your laundry just peed all over the back seat," she whispered.

If it wasn't for her gently building laughter, he would surely have died of embarrassment, then and there. If it wasn't for her gentle laughter, he might have thrown the car in park and ran all the way home. If it wasn't for her gentle laughter, Bartley Farrow might never have rediscovered his humanity.

Instead, he began to laugh with her. Hesitantly at first. Then with loud, broad chuckles. He laughed so hard, he had trouble breathing. And her laughter washed over him like the promise of redemption.

As he drove, Angel deftly untied the tricky knot, freeing the frightened dog from its duffel bag prison. She laughed as it licked her face in joy and confused gratitude. She held Dustball up so it licked Bartley's ear with similar enthusiasm, and they both laughed some more.

Their laughter faded to a cozy silence, more intimate than he had ever experienced. They drove this way for seven more miles, until she pointed to an empty park on the right.

"You can let me off here." she said. With those words, Bartley felt his last chance at life being ripped away from him. He pulled over to the curb, wishing he could find an excuse for talking to her a little longer.

He couldn't.

She opened the passenger's side door and tossed her backpack on the sidewalk.

"Thanks," she said. And as she looked back at him, their eyes met for the briefest of eternities. He bared his soul to her in that one glance. Everything he felt, he feared, he wished for, everything he was, slowly congealed into that single, shared moment. A tear began to escape down his cheek, but he did not feel embarrassed. He knew she would not think less of him. He tried desperately to speak, anything to make the moment last longer.

"Can I..?" but she put her finger to his lips to stop him.

Then, she replaced the finger with her own lips; soft, fluttering and alive. He tasted the kiss of this strange woman in his soul, and the tears fell more quickly.

"Go home to your wife and kids, Bartley Farrow," she said with a tenderness he would never forget. As she stepped out of the car, Dustball pranced after her. Angel picked up the old dog, kissed its furry head, and held it up to the open window.

"You want your laundry back?" she smiled.

Bartley surprised himself by nodding. She gently placed Dustball in the passenger's seat, and calmed the grateful dog with a scratch behind its ear.

"He pees because he thinks you don't love him," she said as she fastened the seatbelt loosely around Dustball.

And with those final words, she was off, slipping away into the cleansing silver moonlight.

Bartley did not watch her go. He didn't have to. He rolled down his window, and stared silently at what was left of his world.

Then, Bartley Farrow turned his aging minivan around with a reckless spin, and began the long journey back home.

Meeting Delilah

"Did ya ever meet a lady that could knock your heart clear up to your throat the first time you set eyes on her? I mean a lady so fine that every time you think of her...your teeth start to sweat?

Now, Delilah...she was that kind of woman.

I remember the first time I ran into Delilah was at the corner grocery store. Actually, she ran into me... Bashed me a good one from behind with a shopping cart, and sent me sprawling face first into one of them there gol-darn feminine hygiene displays!

Now, like any red-blooded, pick-up driving, country boy, I'd rather gnaw off my own arm than get within shiverin' distance of all them lady things. But here I was, wallowing like a pig in mud in a big old pile of clamp-ons, panty liners and I don't even want to know what else!

Let me tell ya, I was not a happy camper.

So's I throw off all those dainty lady things, and scramble up to my feet. I stand there and give her a look that could boil homemade whiskey...and you know what she goes and says to me?

"Excuse me," she says!

That's right. She just looked me square in the face and said, "Excuse me," with the sweetest little voice that ever tickled your eardrums.

"Do what?!" I hollered, madder 'n any wet hen.

"Excuse me..." she says again, tryin' her darndest not to laugh.

Now, ya gotta picture what's happenin' here. I'm feelin' mean and lookin' to punch somebody's lights out for makin' me look like a dang fool in a grocery store aisle; when this lady, she just up and giggles right in my big old red face!

And just like that...my teeth start to sweat!

I mean, I was a goner in no time flat. I woulda dove right back into those Maxipads and Stay-Put doojiggies just to hear her say "Excuse me" again with that silky sweet voice of hers...

But, heck before I know'd whats hit me, she's off in dairy products, and there's some ninety-two year-old stockboy looking at me like I was a pervert, on account of I got a couple of those feminine thingamajigs still wedged in my boots!

They asked me...very politely...never to shop at the Piggly-Wiggly again. And I never have.

Anyways, it took about a week of askin' around town before I finally found out her name was Delilah, and that she worked at the Red Cross blood donation center down past Horton Street.

It took me four pints of blood before I even got up the nerve to ask her out on a date.

I figure I gave up another three or four gallons before I finally convinced her to marry me.

So that's the tale of Delilah and me. We been married 'bout six months now. And you know what? That little filly still makes my teeth sweat.

But the funny thing is... Every darn time I go to kiss her, I still get this confounded urge to roll up my sleeve.

Ain't that a hoot?!"

HIS EYES

Anxiety penetrated the early morning darkness with a thousand disconnected pincers of thought cascading into her consciousness, hovering between receding sleep and the dismal threat of another rapidly encroaching dawn.

Rebecca Matheson, 41, lay with her back pressed into the warm mattress, and stared with desperate eyes at the bedroom ceiling she knew hung somewhere in the vague dimness above her. She didn't have to see it to feel its constraints, to be aware of the harsh limits it imposed on her life. In the too-familiar idleness between reality and slumber which began to consume ever greater parts of her day, she imagined it was that unseen barrier alone which held her now to the bed, as if it alone prevented her from rising up like a suddenly freed balloon, slipping from possessive fingers, and escaping to sweet uncharted oblivion in the wild upper reaches of the wind. Yet like the balloon, the image escaped her now, and she felt the hard ceiling and rigid walls, the stifling darkness and the pressing loneliness of the king-sized bed once more define the boundaries of her life, her hope, her night.

Rebecca imagined she could almost hear the rapid click of the computer keys through closed doors, mocking her from the downstairs den, for it was there that Gregory, her husband of half her adulthood, chose to squander the early hours of his night, time that was once spent with his arms around her, protecting her from her own unbridled fantasies. Now he closed each day isolated, his face painted by the blue-white flicker of a computer monitor, his eyes soaking in lewd images of other people's passion captured in the electronic dust of internet pornography. He made no secret of his obsession with this all-consuming hobby, or the joyless thrill it gave him to seek out, download and permanently store these images in the dark confines of his hard drive. These digital moments of desire, captured, numbered and filed, to be called up at will as an accessibly hollow approximation of human contact, were all he allowed himself now. She smiled at the symbolism of all those writhing couples frozen forever in ethereal memory for her husband's amusement. As she heard the clear, mournful beep of the computer shutting down, and then his soft steps on the carpeted stairs, Rebecca suddenly felt she was married to a specter, who drifted unfettered, unencumbered and unconcerned, between the downstairs den and his far distant corner of the bed.

The bedroom door creaked open behind him, although no light accompanied him into the room. Another symbolism. She heard him try to sneak silently past, though he knew she was awake. Despite his distance, she never actually slept until he was back in bed with her, and he knew that too; yet they each played out their nightly ritual of deeds left unspoken, questions better unasked, conversations never meant to be.

Tonight, however, she could not restrain herself. She had to reach out to him, cut through the separating darkness and deceitful silence, to remind the man she had married that she was still here, anxious and alive, a drowning segment of a woman he had once vowed to cherish forever. So many words and hopes and cries welled up in her, that she was increasingly afraid she would burst into one of her scenes; the ones that always embarrassed him so. As always, the ice-tinged memory of his disapproval of any expression of neediness threw cold water on her desperation, causing it to recede once more into the silent chambers of her soul.

"Did you say something, Bec?" he whispered, and she realized she must have, though she had no idea what thoughts, or how many words escaped her tensed lips.

"You okay?" was all she could think to offer in reply.

"Yeah. Just had a little work to do on the computer. Give me a few minutes." And with that, he fled into the bathroom, leaving her thankfully alone once more. She listened to him brush, spit and brush again, imagined the water swirling from faucet to sink, before escaping down the drain to go who knows where? She heard the flutter of discarded clothes, the complaint of the fifty-year old floor, a flush, a slam, a yawn and the whisper-creak as he finally returned to the bedroom. She felt the mattress rise and steady under his weight, a tug of sheets, and the cool kiss of night air on her now uncovered legs.

"G'night, Bec." he muttered to his pillow.

"G'night, Greg," she returned, his back and miles of mattress between them, as Rebecca Matheson, age 41, closed her eyes and dreamt of drifting balloons and free flowing water.

****

Despite her best efforts, and though she hated to admit it even to herself, Rebecca had long ago stopped seeing her husband as a person. Instead, he became little more than an amalgamation of annoyances, a personification of all those maddening little habits, clichés and failings which were once obscured by affection. He was never Gregory anymore. He was that irritating click of sinuses all through the night. He was the toothpaste smudge on the bathroom sink, which could have been so easily washed away, but wasn't. He was underwear on the floor, endless football games on TV, dirty dishes caked with dry grease, condescending looks and continual grunts of disapproval. He was burps and farts and embarrassing sounds never made while they were dating. Even worse, he was the inattentive ear that no longer cared about her fears and troubles; the soft word of compassion freely uttered to strangers, but never to her anymore; the strong, comforting arm that once wrapped so deliciously around her while she slept, but now remained on his side of the bed, an entire, empty marriage away.

Inevitably, her mind began to wander into dangerous spaces, in search of shadows of emotions she yearned to remember.

In this way, she had slowly come to understand that affairs are seldom about sex alone. On the contrary, sex was merely the mechanism, not the goal, like a jet which lifts you off the ground and tosses you giddily through the air, yet it is not the engine but the desire to reach that distant, half-remembered city which really begins your journey and ultimately defines it. She began to see an affair as a gradual snap of judgment and idealism; a sudden, unfolding shock to the system; a breathless realization that there is at least one person left in the world who, despite all, still finds you fascinating...desirable...or simply above contempt; an unexpected and desperate oasis in the vast, searing desert of 'it's all your fault.'

To be truthful, neither of them had wanted the relationship to dwindle, nor had expected it to fall apart so quickly. Yet as it unraveled, neither had the willingness to endure the thousand weekly irritations which gnawed at their marriage. They learned it is better to save up your contempt for the big battles and postpone the small, just as it is easier to defend against a lion's sudden onslaught than the constant swarm of mosquitoes, even though after days and years of winged attack, an equal amount of blood might be drained from the living.

And so it was between them, bloodless, cold to the point of politeness. And as she fell into a restless sleep, Rebecca Matheson felt the soft shredding of her heart.

****

Their morning rites were equally well-established, as each jostled for the shower, the towels, the sink. Two out-of-sync dancers sharing the same steps with different rhythms and cross-purposes. Under the first blush of new marriage, they showered together at every opportunity. Now the very idea was dismissed out of hand as a foolishly inefficient waste of time.

Over the course of sixteen years, their names had atomized along with their relationship. She had gone from Rebecca, to Becca to Bec. He had slipped from Gregory to Greg, to not even being named at all for whole weeks of interaction.

And so it went, year after year, argument after argument, hemorrhaging humanity within the very institutional relationship each had once believed in so fervently.

Perhaps if they had been able to have children; perhaps that might have filled the empty gnawing void between them. Instead, the vultures of silent accusation hovered continuously, and swooped down on them at moments of fatigue and vulnerability to poke and tear at any shred of intimacy which remained in the sparse conversations they shared. They were left, emotional carrion, because of a simple flaw in their ability to reproduce.

Yet, the idea of raising children also brought shudders from Rebecca, as it raised the specter of her own tragic upbringing.

Her mother, with her charming French accent and fiery Parisian temper, had been the stability in young Rebecca's life. It was she who taught Rebecca that men were the detestable and expendable half of the human equation. Her father had been a pilot, a man who routinely left as a profession. Yet, every time he took off carried the promise of a return, and always with a small toy, stuffed animal or souvenir from some distant city. She had seven prized bears from Chicago alone, and her collection of brass Empire State Buildings, plastic Golden Gate bridges and pewter St. Louis arches was the finest in the neighborhood. Her daddy would fly away and her little heart would break, but he would land, days later, and the wound would come close to healing. On the other hand, when her mother finally took off, she departed for good. A spontaneous flight to the land of her birth, the country and culture that had been gradually wrung out of her by long years as a middle-class American wife; until one day, when Rebecca was eleven, the urge to return became overpowering for her mother, and she could do nothing but surrender to it. She bought a one-way ticket with her husband's frequent flyer miles, and other than an occasional postcard, removed herself from her daughter's life for good.

Left without anyone to raise his daughter, Rebecca's father was forced to quit the profession that defined him, the job he loved. He transferred from cockpit to cubicle, and a little bit of him died each day, weighted down by drab gray furniture and the white plaster ceiling between him and the sky he once conquered. Gone was the adrenaline infused dash down a runway, hurling a hunk of metal the approximate size and weight of a building straight into the air. His days were now built around e-mail and paper clips and figures on a page which reduced the excitement of flight to meaningless calculations of cargo tonnage and revenue generated.

Rebecca watched her father wither with responsibility, and realized her mother had taken more than a few pieces of clothing with her to France, she had also taken the better part of two other lives.

Seeing no refuge in past or present, Rebecca's vision of the future resembled a windshield increasingly obscured by the splattered remains of long hours on a sorrow-encrusted highway.

Fortunately, she had her job to occupy her days. A short subway trip packed in with the smells and shoves of impolite strangers, then a revolving door into a cold glass and steel monolith, a crowded elevator ride where everyone struggled to withhold words, and finally into her tiny isolated cubicle, where she felt more in control than anywhere else in her life. There were no doors here, but there were distractions. It was not a career. What she did was tediously unimportant, as much to her as to whomever she tried to describe her job. Yet, here she at least belonged, had purpose, could do something right, no matter how trivial. It was the same with most of her friends, who realized, but seldom admitted, that work was the therapeutic oasis of modern life; a grinding, decades-long diversion; a temporarily imposed dose of sanity for the terminally unfulfilled.

It felt safer to put in her hours at work before she was forced to face the more terrifying prospect of putting in her hours at home.

****

And so it was on this particular afternoon, that Rebecca Matheson hid within the comforting anonymity of the after-work crowd, belching its way into the yellowing tiled expanse of the subway terminal. She stood apart and watched car after car pass, emptying, filling and departing again as quickly as it arrived, and she wondered briefly how absurd this numbed procession would appear to any who occupied this city centuries ago, or even to those who had designed the first subways with wistful visions of luxury   and   convenience.

While she leaned against a square-tiled pillar, studying the ebb and flow of blank-faced humanity, her gaze flittered and found a single face, oozing turmoil and emotion. He looked vaguely familiar, as if she had seen those eyes before, only now they were distant, wild and tortured, peering through his sweat-soaked hair like a glimpse of fire raging behind the tree line.

She could not escape his eyes. They didn't rest on anything in particular, but seemed to soak in all the visual cacophony at once; as someone watching a parade of ants does not pick out a single insect, but rather takes in the wave-like progression of the swarm; or the way a field of flowing grass seduces the eye into absorbing the overall pattern of motion, while overlooking each individual blade of grass.

She watched him seeing, and saw something more, something profoundly disturbing. Something about the frantic humanity of his gaze, the haunted, pleading look in his eyes that resonated in an empty part of her chest, until she too felt like crying or screaming or both.

The stranger appeared lost, dazed, and in considerable pain. He could have been one of a dozen suffering crack addicts who staggered and bleared their way, ghost-like, through the subway station, but she knew somehow, he wasn't. It was the way he stood, the way he moved, as if he had been abruptly broken, not worn or shriveled by years of chemical succor.

Despite his haggard appearance, he seemed to her a handsome man. Tall and gaunt, with that mystical Van Gough quality she had always found so attractive. She imagined him a writer or an artist, tortured by his own creative passions. She watched as he moved against the crowd, a lone lemming cursed with sudden insight, frantically trying to jump species before the mass plunge into oblivion.

Nothing seemed to be connected. He didn't move from one space to another, or even one moment to the next, but merely appeared, as if he were unable to remember where he was, or where he was going. She watched him stand before a train door, which appeared out of the darkness and screeched angrily to a stop by his feet, disgorged its human contents, and waited expectantly for him to be sucked into its metal confines with a swell of others. Yet, he did not move. Instead, the ethereal stranger stared at the insistent opening, until offended and angry, the doors closed before him, and the train fled further down the darkened tunnel.

Suddenly, he stood alone on the platform, the crush of humanity having left him stranded and gasping in its determined wake.

Rebecca realized she should have been on that train also, but was so caught up in studying this desperate wanderer, she had forgotten the train's purpose in transporting her home.

Aside from the two of them, the terminal was empty.

They were together alone, the lost soul and the fascinated observer.

She watched him struggle for breath, as his eyes seemed to fix on the empty subway tracks. She gasped as he slowly, methodically, stepped toward the tiled cliff, the lemming who chose to surrender to centuries of instinct, rather than live with the dreadful plague of self-awareness.

The tall, distraught man took another short, staggering step forward, until his toes kissed the open air at the edge of the subway platform.

One more moment and he would be gone. He either did not hear or chose to ignore the echoing clatter of a distant oncoming train, but the screech and clatter propelled her now, the curious observer no more.

Before his feet could take that final step, she grabbed his forearm and changed her life forever, her hand burning coolly against his fevered skin.

With dazed and desperate eyes, he looked up from her hand to her face, as if noticing another human on the planet for the very first time. She watched as he studied her, and suddenly felt it was actually she, who was the desperate one, she, who was the soul in turmoil teetering on the edge of a platform. In that shared look, the absurdity of her life welled up to meet the anguish of his, until they each trembled under the silent accusation of communal emptiness.

Without removing her hand from his arm, she studied his face intently, searching deep within him; for what, she did not know. Then her eyes softened in embarrassment at her own anxious intrusion, and the smile that crinkled her lips was tinged with sadness.

"That's not the way home," was all she could say, though her words lacked commitment. "That's not the way. Believe me."

Rebecca Matheson, 41, was unable to remove her hand from the stranger's arm, as she led him away from the lure of the subway tracks to the safety of the staircase. As the next train arrived and the station filled once again, he let her lead him like a child out of the terminal, up to the roaring street, and into the cool embrace of the night air.

She clung to his arm as he leaned on her for support. He might have been dangerous, an addict on the edge, or an escapee from some facility for the criminally insane, but she knew in her soul he wasn't, and even if he was, part of her no longer cared. There were tears in her eyes, as she felt his frightened trust hit her like a falling safe. No one had ever trusted her in her entire life. Not her father who bought off his absence with stuffed toys. Not her mother her could not see in her daughter a reason to remain. No one had ever depended on her. Not her shell of a husband who depended more on digitally induced stimulation than marital interaction. No one had ever let her lead them like this fevered stranger with the haunted and haunting eyes. All her life, she had been buffeted by the actions of others, reacting instead of living. But this man, this troubled, enigmatic stranger, allowed her to look beyond her own sorrow and inadequacies for the first time in years. And she was found a reason to flourish in that brief moment of connection.

She let him go only long enough to flag down a taxi. The overweight Turkish cabby looked with disgust at her sweating companion, he had endured too many winos and addicts in his time. She pleaded fervently with the driver to take her passenger to the local clinic, and finally had to offer him a fifty dollar tip for the eleven block ride before he grumbled a surly agreement.

She turned back to the stranger now, as he stood wavering on the sidewalk, looking as if he would crumple at the slightest word. She smiled, as one who has crumpled too many times herself, and opened the rear passenger side door of the taxi. Without a word, she gently helped him inside. He watched in confusion as she handed the burly driver the estimated fare, plus a crumpled fifty. Then she turned to him, to stare once more into those painfully expressive eyes.

"You have a fever," she whispered. "It feels like a bad one. The cabdriver will take you to the hospital now. They will take care of you there."

He moved his mouth to speak, but chose not to, jarring her instead with his perceptive silence. His eyes peered straight through to her soul, and Rebecca felt suddenly vulnerable and ashamed; ashamed not for what she had done, but for what she hadn't done, not for those things she had risked, but for all that she had settled for, bit by bit, in her life up to that point; for each of the dreams, hopes and passions she had gradually and systematically compromised; until slowly, insidiously, she was left only a hollow, screaming voice buried deep within what should have been someone else's existence. This was the terrible, freeing effect his eyes had on her; they wrenched her out of that numbed complacency she had hidden within ever since her mother abandoned her so many tears ago.

Her hand brushed the sweat-soaked hair from his forehead, then rested on his cheek with a soft caress.

She searched his eyes once again, again she felt embarrassed by her own anxious intrusion. And again, she smiled reassuringly.

"I'm sorry," she murmured. Sorry for not jumping in the cab with him. Sorry for not living up to the trust she saw in his eyes. Sorry for the hungry void he seemed to sense in her. Impulsively, she planted a kiss on his damp forehead, then stepped back, closed the cab door, and watched as the taxi pulled away into the swirling snarl of traffic.

She stood there silently, until the taxi was an indistinct yellow blur in a distant river of movement and sound. Then she slowly turned back to the waiting subway station and the life from which she had been granted a temporary and unexpected reprieve.

As she descended the concrete steps into the bowels of the subway station, Rebecca Matheson sadly wondered if she would ever have the opportunity to lose herself in those haunting eyes again.

WITHOUT HER

It had been seven months since she left him.

Seven months, thirteen days, eleven hours, and an infinite number of nights spent staring at the ceiling, cursing his fate, cursing himself, cursing her.

During that time, he had grown bitter in barely noticed increments, as the joy quietly drained from each moment spent alone. Restaurants lost their flavor, because she was not along to sample their delicacies. The theater offered no distraction, because her season ticket left an empty chair at his right elbow, which overpowered every performance with its silent accusations and melancholy. The park, the hiking trails and the botanical gardens she loved so much were suddenly overgrown with sadness, so that each of her favorite flowers became a mere mockery of beauty, a fragrant gash hemorrhaging color and impermanence. Even reading, his lifelong escape and passion, held no solace. After she left, he re-read all his favorite novels with furious abandon, and found them, like himself, empty and lifeless. His familiar books closed their dry whispery pages around him like a tomb. When she left, she had even taken this with her, leaving him no interest, no mirth, nowhere to hide.

Had she taken all the enjoyment from his life, or had he squeezed it out himself? In the end, it hardly mattered. Cynicism and self-pity were the only luxuries he allowed himself these days.

He had gradually isolated himself from friends, first with excuses, then negligence, and finally rudeness. He was not a cruel man, but he became unable to separate her friends from his, and if they were even partially hers, they hurt his eyes like the brilliant stab of sunlight after one emerges from a comfortably darkened room.

There had been many calls, of course. Words of comfort, condolence and commiseration. Most were heartfelt, but each came with a price. Each caller expected him to eventually emerge from the depths, and he simply did not want to. After a few weeks, their tone subtly changed. As weeks became months, their growing impatience slipped between words and pauses, and could not be hidden by insulating clichés.

She's gone.

You have to accept it.

It's time to move on.

You have to get on with your life.

They did not want to hear the desperate truth; that he had no life left in him. They were embarrassed and uncomfortable before the depths of his anger and undiminishing loss.

To hell with them, he thought. I have better things to do than feign bravery for those would-be consolers.

Of course, any better things he had to do were frustratingly difficult to identify. Today, he found himself standing by the kitchen counter, angrily smearing mayonnaise on a gray slab of processed turkey in a pitiful attempt at dinner. As he slapped together his sandwich, he talked to her, just as he had done when he used to create all those marvelously complex gourmet delights for her, the kitchen suffused in the inviting aroma of sautéed garlic, onion and ginger. But this time, she was not standing by the sink beside him, laughing with him, admiring his culinary skills, sharing his passion, his life.

He slowly dropped the mayonnaise knife and closed his eyes, so he could see her there once more. The sparkle of her eyes, green today, perhaps hazel tomorrow. Her unnaturally natural red hair pulled back severely, in direct contrast to the ease of her laughter. She was forever laughing, one of those rare gem-like people who could uncover humor in anything, including his own dour personality. Her laughter poured out with sparkling tones that filled any room with her presence. It was deeply contagious and would frequently rescue him from his tendency towards self-importance.

He remembered her skin; soft, slightly freckled, with a pale golden hue which ignited the fire in her ever-changing eyes. He raised his hand slightly to touch a cheek that wasn't there, then let if fall once again to his side, heavy with disappointment.

He remembered her lips, so distinctive, so seductive. Many times, as she spoke to him in her rapid, excited manner, he would lose her sentences because he was so captivated by the sculptured beauty of her smile. Almost against his will, his gaze would sneak down to her wide, red lips and watch as they danced and played with every word that poured out from her too-perfect mouth. She would catch him not listening, and happily berate him for his inattention.

"You have the attention span of an amnesiac ant," she would tease, and he would again lose himself in the loving embrace of her laughter.

But she embraced him no longer.

With no appetite to speak of, he flung the uneaten pressed turkey sandwich into the sink, then crossed into the silent living room to seek out the meager solace of his old recliner. As he lowered himself to its worn cushions, he remembered her form, her elegance, the way she moved.

He had thought her scrawny when he first met her, fairy-like in her small, delicate frame. His opinion changed when she outran him by two miles the first time he was foolish enough to accept her invitation to go jogging together. He had always appreciated the full, generous curves of a woman, but gradually began to consider anything less than this vibrant, wispy shape as something less than feminine. The vitality he discovered within her changed his very definition of what beauty should be. Now beauty was only found in smooth, thin legs, tiny breasts, and a neck as subtle and graceful as a swan. She would often joke that she wanted her breasts implanted with automobile airbags, so he could then have a real woman on demand; and they would laugh, and he would sputter clumsily that she was the most perfect woman he had ever seen, and she would laugh again in appreciation and total disbelief.

He imagined her smell now; the soft, subtle perfume which graced her neck every day he was with her. He remembered the electric shudder when he touched the silky smoothness of her thighs. He remembered how she kissed him, and how he would lose himself so fully in her arms. Those tiny arms sheltered him from all the worries he had piled on his shoulders over the years. Those tiny arms were a haven, but his haven no more, and he hated her for taking them away from him.

She could have fought more.

She could have resisted.

Not everyone succumbs, and even the doctors were surprised at how quickly she dwindled.

Only three months, instead of the years predicted, or the lifetime promised.

If she really loved him, she would have fought harder.

"If you really loved me...!" he screamed to the empty room, before his hot, angry tears choked the words in his throat.

He pulled his aching knees to his chest, curled up in his chair, and wept bitterly for nearly half an hour. He pictured her berating him for this pitiful act of self-indulgence, and even her imagined criticism brought some degree of comfort.

"It's time to get on with your life," his eldest son had told him on the phone yesterday. "Mom would have wanted it that way."

Maybe he was right.

Maybe it was time to crawl back to the surface again. He knew she would have wanted him to.

But then again, it had only been seven months.

Seven months, thirteen days, twelve hours, and an infinite number of nights spent staring up at the ceiling...

NASHVILLE

The door to the penthouse of Nashville's famed Coleridge Tower flew open, and LG. Munroe, a fast-talking executive in an exquisitely tailored Italian suit shoved the tall, denim-clad singer into his luxurious suite of offices.

"So that's the bum's rush tour, Bobby Ray," Munroe summed up with feigned indifference. "Twenty-two floors of state-of-the-art, star-making machinery. Impressed?"

After too many gigs played in trailer parks and street corner dives, Bobby Ray Burton couldn't help but be drawn to the rows of gold and platinum albums which lined the walls. "Well, I..." he sputtered.

Munroe happily slapped the young singer on the shoulder and ushered him deeper into the office. "'Course you're impressed, boy. This is country music heaven! And I just gave you a back stage pass to the Pearly Gates!"

Bobby Ray scanned each of the thirty-five framed photographs of the famed promoter beside him frozen in time with country music's biggest stars.

"Tell the truth, I'm a might bit...overwhelmed," Bobby Ray sputtered.

"That's why we do it like this, kid," Munroe elbowed him conspiratorially. "We could probably get the same amount of work done on a floor and a half, but who the hell would be overwhelmed with that?"

"I see what you mean."

"Image is everything in this business. Remember that."

"Yes, sir."

"Not that you're any stranger to image, are you, Bobby Ray?" The silver-haired executive fixed him with a stare that made Bobby Ray feel like he was a walking MRI.

Bobby Ray tried on his best easy smile. Under normal circumstances, nothing could shake his composure; he knew he could sing; knew the ladies went wild for his broad chest, tight jeans and black ponytail; and knew in his bones that his songwriting was twice as good as anything on the charts today. But this was Nashville, and here he was in the office of the legendary LG. Munroe; the man who could make or break a career with just the raise of an eyebrow. Bobby Ray suddenly felt like he was tap dancing with rattlers.

"What exactly are you sayin', Mr. Munroe?"

"LG., please." The promoter gestured to an antique Louis XVI chair. "My friends and enemies call me LG. Only my accountant calls me Mr. Munroe." He waited until Bobby Ray lowered himself carefully into the spindly antique, before he plopped his own small form into the oversized executive chair behind his desk, making sure he left an intimidating ocean of mahogany between them.

Bobby Ray smiled weakly as he tried to reposition his long, denim-clad legs in the expensive chair.

"Now, where were we? Oh, yeah... Images. Specifically, your image, Bobby Ray."

"Me? I'm just a poor old country boy lookin' to sing my songs to anyone who'll take the time to listen."

"Now, see? That's your image!" Munroe waved his pale hands expansively. "And everything about you supports that image. The pre-faded jeans and cowboy boots. The old, worn guitar...even the trademark baby blue cowboy hat!"

"I make no apologies for what I am, Mr. Munroe."

"LG."

"I just want you to know I'm not one of them there vinyl n' tin foil cowboys playin' country music just 'cuz they couldn't make it in rock and roll."

"You're country through and through." Munroe nodded with an uncomfortably wide smile.

"That's a fact."

"A good old boy with good old American values."

"That's what made this country great."

"You probably drive an old Ford pick-up, don't you, kid?"

Now it was Bobby Ray's turn to flash a wicked smile. "It's parked out back. Right next to your Tesla Roadster." He leaned back in his chair, determined not to appear out of place in this temple of country music deification. "Look, Mr. Munroe. I know you're head of this here record company and a real big man in the music business." He knew he had one shot at this; it was important that he choose his words carefully. "But I'm not lookin' to change who or what I am for nobody. I'm Bobby Ray Burton, and that's all I ever wanted to be."

Munroe pursed his lips in thought. "A man of integrity. How refreshing."

"If that means I don't get to be as big a name as Garth or Waylon...I guess that's how it's gotta be then."

"A man who knows himself and is true to his inner core."

Something in Munroe's too-easy smile gave Bobby Ray the impression he was being toyed with, and that set his own teeth on edge. An eerie tension crackled between the two men as they faced each other; the rich, aging promoter and the ambitious young singer; the past demanding its pound of flesh from the future.

"Make no mistake, Mr. Munroe. I'm not gonna change. Not for you, or nobody."

A silence hovered over them, which somehow seemed to shift the gravity in the room towards the veteran promoter. LG. Munroe pressed the tips of his fingers together and tried to fathom the depth of commitment in the younger man's eyes. He had looked across this same expansive desk many times before, stared down hundreds just like this one; carbon-copy cowboys sporting week-old whiskers and in-your-face attitudes, so hungry for immortality, it made his heart weary.

But he had to admit, this kid was tougher than most.

"And who'd want you to change?" he sighed at last. Then he reached down into his top desk drawer and pulled out a well-handled manila file. The label on the file read: BURTON, BOBBY RAY.

From across the massive desk, the cowboy crooner watched the eyes of the promoter dart across the various pages condensing his life to sentences and statistics. He desperately wished he could see what words the faceless writers had chosen to sum up his talent, his future.

"As it happens, I've been following your career for months, Bobby Ray," Munroe intoned, as if he was reviewing an errant child's report card. "You're beginning to develop a small, but loyal following. You just put out a CD on a tiny indie label. You have four songs you wrote yourself..."

"Five. I'm mostly finished with my fifth. It's a love song about this woman I've been seein'."

"Sad song, I hope."

"Beg pardon?"

"Come on now, Bobby Ray. This is country music! You know love songs dipped in tears sell the best." His eyes soaked in the details of yet another fact page. "You arrived in Nashville eleven months ago, hitting the small club and bar circuit hoping for your big break."

"You do your homework."

"It's my job. You also told a music reporter in a small Atlanta newspaper that Bobby Ray Burton would rather be, and I quote: 'the kind of man my momma would be proud of, than some plastic-haired, no-talent, country music sell-out.' End quote."

The young singer shrugged, having at last found a comfortable position to make his stand. "It's who I am. Take it or leave it."

Munroe hesitated for only a moment, before he pushed out of his chair and crossed to the wet bar on the opposite corner of the spacious office, strategically placed under the signed pictures of Elvis and Merle Haggard. He poured himself a generous Jack Daniel's, then filled a second glass for Bobby Ray.

"Oh, we'll take it. Bobby Ray," he offered, with gleeful malevolence. "We'll take it all the way to the bank. And you're gonna love the ride, believe me."

"So you lookin' to sign me, then?" Bobby Ray hated his tone for betraying so much. He made up for the thrill in his voice by adopting a disinterested saunter from his chair to LG's side. He shook his hair back and accepted the drink that was shoved into his hand, then listened calmly as the promoter outlined the next few years of his soon-to-be-amazing life.

"We start small. Major album release, with option for three more. Half-million in promotion. Two music videos with the stereotypical blondes in halter tops and Daisy Dukes. Then a year-long national tour, fronting for some big name band. Sound good so far?"

"Sounds about right."

"We'll put press releases in all the trade papers. Book appearances for you on all the major talk shows. And maybe get you in as a presenter on the next Country Music Awards. Create a lot of buzz." He swirled the brown liquid in his glass like a magician. "Still happy?"

"I'm getting' there."

The two men clinked glasses in celebration, then each savored the seductive burn of the aged whiskey. "You don't feel you're compromising your identity with all this success, do you, son?" Munroe cracked a mischievous grin.

"Just 'cuz I'm country, don't mean I don't know a good deal when I see one." Bobby Ray smiled in return, then added, "As long as you take me as I am, then I reckon I'm yours all the way."

With a soft nod of his head, Munroe trotted back to his desk. He pulled a pre-drafted contract from his drawer. Dangled it out in front of Bobby Ray. "Oh, and of course we'll throw in the standard $25,000 signing bonus."

Bobby Ray tossed a roguish wink at his benefactor, as his fingers grabbed the contract. "You're not takin' advantage of me, are you, LG.?"

"I am. Make it $50,000."

It was the moment the young singer had been waiting for, had been dreaming of for more years and in more honky-tonk dives than he cared to remember. His heart pounded in his ears as he flipped through the neatly typed pages. "So where do I sign?"

"The bottoms of page four, seven and nine. Initial each of the other pages at the top."

"You got a pen?"

"Ain't it funny how real cowboys never carry pens?" Munroe raised an eyebrow, and he sent a gold-plated pen skittering across the desk. "Anyway, I suggest you get your lawyers to read it first. I guarantee ours did."

Bobby Ray grabbed the pen and dropped his signature on page four. "No need. You look like an honest man. I trust you."

"I'm glad." Munroe leaned back in his chair. "However, I suggest you read page six, Sub-paragraph seven carefully." The promoter rose, turned away from his new client, as he crossed to the wet bar. "You may find it's not a standard clause in these things."

Munroe poured himself another Jack, his back strategically aimed at Bobby Ray's face. He did not have to see him to know what would happen when he read the paragraph in question.

"What in hell...?"

"Read it carefully, junior."

"This some kind of joke, or somethin'?!"

When Munroe turned back around, any last vestige of pleasantry had drained from his weary expression. "No, Bobby Ray. It's no joke. It's an iron-clad, got-you-by-the-balls contract that will make your career if you sign it... Or leave you warbling to a bunch of bored drunks for twenty bucks a night if you don't." He swirled his drink one more time. "The choice is yours."

"This is bullshit!"

"Sub-paragraph seven? No. It's a legitimate business arrangement. I make you a star..." Munroe turned away again and took a long swallow from his glass, before slamming it down on the bar. "And you agree...in writing...to stay the hell away from my wife."

Bobby Ray tossed the contract across the desk. He stood and stomped menacingly over to the older man.

"I oughta kick your ass!"

"Or I should kick yours, don't you think?" The room was bathed in liquid hatred as LG. Munroe stared up into the glaring eyes of his wife's burly lover. Finally, he stepped out from under from the younger man's scarcely restrained fury, and returned to the familiar safety of his ornate desk. "However, this contract will accomplish pretty much the same thing. I want you to keep your hands and your...other things...off my wife. And because I love Crystal, I'm willing to take some no-talent country gigolo and make him a star. If, and only if, he breaks off this tawdry little affair before she gets hurt."

"She ain't gonna get hurt."

Munroe nodded. "I'm here to see she doesn't. According to the clause in question; you call her up... Tell her you found some other bimbo. And then never see, or contact her again. If you do, you agree to return seventy-five percent of all royalties you earn on your next four albums back to me." His eyes narrowed on the young cowboy. "Of course, if you really do love her like you say, losing all that fame and fortune won't matter much to you, will it, son?"

It took only four steps for Bobby Ray to dive across the massive desk and slam LG. Munroe against the wall, his forearm wedged heavily against the older man's windpipe.

"Now I see why Crystal hates you so much! You're nothing but a manipulating little sonofabitch!"

"Unlike you," Munroe gasped, his face purpling. "You love her for her mind...not her husband's position with the largest country music label in the world."

"I'm gonna break your neck!"

"That's...that's your choice," he wheezed. "But if you do, I assure you, no one else on this label, or anywhere in Nashville, has any intention of signing that contract. They all know how much talent you really have."

Bobby Ray sneered into Munroe's bulging eyes. Purple-faced and gasping for breath, the music promoter hung there on the wall, a tragic piece of emotional art pinioned under the frozen smiles of country's biggest names.

After a long moment of indecision, Bobby Ray stepped backwards, letting the older man crash to the floor.

"This is blackmail!"

"No," LG. whispered hoarsely, as he rubbed his neck and struggled to sit up against the wall. "This is a simple man with a star-struck wife, doing what he has to do to survive. A man who can't compete anymore with your kind...all you wannabe country stars who don't mind using some poor, aging woman who can't help falling for any young stud with a guitar and tight Levi's."

Now it was Bobby Ray's turn to face the bar. "It's not like that with me and Crystal," he said softly.

"Then prove me wrong, kid. Tear up the contract."

Ignoring the pain which outraged his elbows, hip and chest, LG Munroe slowly pulled himself up against the wall. Once he felt his legs might not betray him, he leaned against the heavy desktop and tried to straighten his silver hair with trembling fingers. He refused to sit, though his injured frame screamed at him to accept the comfort of the chair. He glared with disdainful pride at the younger man's broad back, then winced as he pictured Crystal wrapped so eagerly around it.

"Gimme a couple of days to think this over," Bobby Ray mumbled.

"You've got an hour."

With a heavy breath of contempt, Bobby Ray turned back to face LG. As he tramped toward the desk, neither man knew if his intent would be violence or concession. At the last moment, the cowboy snatched the contract and stomped toward the office door.

His hand was almost on the doorknob, when LG. began to read aloud from his file.

"Bobby Ray Burton... Real name -- Martin Harold Borelski." The young man froze at the door, as LG. continued his narration.

"Borelski was born and raised in Cambridge, Massachusetts. Father was an economics professor at MIT. Young Martin holds a Master's Degree in Theater from Bentley College. The closest he ever got to a ranch was on a fifth-grade field trip."

Slowly, Bobby Ray turned to face his accuser.

"The man who has to be true to who he is," Munroe sneered. "Your fans are going to absolutely love this."

Bobby Ray tramped the long stretch of carpet to the mahogany desk. His voice was dipped in disgust, as he leaned over. He grabbed the pen like a weapon, as he signed the contract on the bottom of pages four and seven.

"Say good-bye to Crystal for me."

"The contract allows you to you say good-bye yourself."

He scrawled 'Bobby Ray Burton' on the bottom of page nine, initialed the others, then tossed the contract and the gold pen on the desk.

"What's the point?" he shrugged.

Munroe nodded.

"Welcome to Nashville, Bobby Ray."

Without another word, Bobby Ray Burton stomped out of the office, and into the lucrative client roster of Nashville's most powerful record company. Once he was gone, his benefactor slunk back into the safety of his plush, high-back chair. He rubbed his aching throat, then pressed the intercom button on his telephone.

A woman's voice chirped back over the speaker phone. "Yes, Mr. Munroe?"

"Marie, I've got another contract to go in my...special file. Kid calls himself Bobby Ray Burton."

"Oh..." even the electronic circuitry couldn't disguise the pity in her tone. "I'm so, sorry, Mr. Munroe."

"Thanks, Marie." He sucked in a deep, staccato breath that somehow failed to fill his lungs. "Uh...you know the process. Call promotions. Notify our best songwriters. And let's get someone to teach this kid to sing, okay?"

"Yes, sir." A sympathetic pause. "Anything else, Mr. Munroe?"

"Yeah." He hesitated. Smoothed back his silver hair. "See if you can get my wife on the phone for me."

"Yes, sir."

In the silence that followed, LG. Munroe, superstar promoter and country music legend, leaned back in his chair to keep from spilling tears on the large mahogany desk that represented his last place of refuge.

PHILANTHROPY

The darkly tinted windows in the back seat of the steel-gray stretch limousine provided the optimal vantage point for communing with the teeming globs of humanity he dearly loved; so perfect a view, in fact, that multi-billionaire Bryce Townsend IV was tempted to ask his driver to slow down, in order that he could savor this moment with his people.

He eased the embossed receiver from its hidden indentation in the aged oak and leather door, and smiled at the eager response which came through the telephone even before it reached his ear.

"Yes, Mr. Townsend?"

"Edgar," he whispered excitedly into the device. "Could you pull over to the curb for a moment?"

"Is everything all right, sir?"

"Yes, Edgar. Pull over."

"I beg your pardon, Mr. Townsend, but this isn't the safest of neighborhoods..."

"Now, Edgar!" He hated being questioned, even by such a loyal employee as his chauffeur, who had served the famed philanthropist for the last three decades. "I want to see them now!"

"The people, sir?"

"Yes, aren't they magnificent?"

Edgar didn't answer. In truth, he would have been unable to answer in any form that would have satisfied Bryce Townsend IV.

For Edgar, the son of a dedicated Teamster, who had been shot to death by his co-workers for crossing a picket line, had lost the ability to find any unvarnished splendor in those on the bottom floors of society. To him, there was little nobility in their disgruntled toil, no poetry in their menacing glances, and no grandeur in their trudging steps of weariness and contempt. These were his people, and it is notoriously hard to recognize angels after one has smoked with them, shot pool with them, and drank with them through all those Saturday night gatherings of communal chest-thumping and self-delusion.

Bryce, on the other hand, could admire the inherent saintliness of the species precisely because he kept himself so far removed from them, in the same way a visitor to an art museum might gush long and eloquently over the deep meaning evoked by a painting, which has absolutely no basis in what the artist really intended to say. Within the comfortable confines of his sheltered world, poverty was unseen, and therefore something dark and exciting. And to the truly disconnected, it is a but a small leap from the exciting to the admirable.

And so degradation becomes virtue -- destitution, saintliness.

Bryce Townsend IV had grown up amidst a flurry of hired nannies and appointed tutors. Although he would never ever need to earn a living, he became an accomplished writer, self-publishing three novels which explored the human condition from the enviable position of impartial observer. Writing was his shield, philanthropy his kindly retreat. He had always voted for Liberal Democrats because, like him, they were the champions of the underclass and disadvantaged, especially when it meant they seldom had to mingle or cross paths with any of the wretched souls. Newspapers, a few of which he owned, praised his generosity for incorporating well-appointed homeless shelters within five miles of every office complex he built. The city fathers honored him for contributing to a score of charities and worthy causes, including Planned Parenthood, The Nation of Islam, and the National Endowment For The Arts.

One Christmas Eve, he had instructed Edgar to place one hundred dollar bills in each of the Salvation Army Santa cauldrons all over town. He would have gone with his uniformed chauffeur that festive night, but he felt it might have attracted too much attention, besides which it was too beastly cold to be doing charity out of doors.

He had even donated two copies of each of his novels to every library and secondary school in the state.

Now, as the limo silently idled by the curbside, Bryce glowed inwardly at the ragged throngs who stared back at his darkened windows, before scurrying off to their tiny mortgaged homes, their flickering TV sets, and their faltering marriages. He imagined that if only they knew who was behind the darkly tinted glass, how grateful they would be for all he had done for them. Didn't he donate that huge bronze replica of Rodan's

Thinker to the Wycast-Burnuck Housing Project? Didn't he underwrite that Mapplethorpe art exhibit at the local junior high school? They would be so eager to shake his hand, that is, if he would ever have let them.

He would not, of course. For all their unwashed glory, Bryce would have been appalled by the simplest form of physical contact.

Each night, before she had one of the hired nannies prepare her son for bed, Bryce's mother, Olivia Townsend, had lectured her son on the inappropriateness of physical affection, and how it invaded the all-important privacy of a truly civilized soul. Bryce's father, Bryce Townsend III, would often call from the family's various estates to warn his son how the common handshake may give off the mistaken impression of equality. Touch was the most primitive and unnecessary of the senses, he was told, and the vast sea of humanity had not evolved very far from the ape-like man who groped and pawed the black monolith. This concept was the ideal balm for the shy and lonely adolescent. When he turned fourteen, one of Bryce's many tutors spent a full semester detailing the hordes of insidious microbes passed through every-day human contact. Needless to say, Bryce's most prized possession were his Caspian black leather gloves.

Yet, isolation is always more tolerable in a silken cocoon. Bryce Townsend IV was handsome, he knew, and richer than most people could even fathom. He was one of the first to count his personal assets in the billions, instead of the more common millions. When his parents were killed in a freak skiing accident in the Swiss Alps, Bryce IV was left in control of an international conglomerate with annual revenues greater than that of most nations in the Southern Hemisphere. He was named the country's most eligible bachelor...a title he did not relish.

As he passed from his teens through his thirties, the concept of physical intimacy paled in appeal. The imagined passions of youth proved to be an awkward and frightful business, easily forgotten and sanitized. One young woman from a very respectable strip mall dynasty had cornered him after college graduation and gratuitously rubbed her well-endowed chest and hips against him, but for some inexplicable reason became offended when he wouldn't remove his gloves to touch her. After that, sex became solely an exercise in mental self-discipline, and he displayed the iron will of a militant ex-smoker. At forty-three, his celibacy was as cherished as his celebrated philanthropy.

Gloves and distance were the rule in the Townsend estate, both the cook and personal physician wore sanitized latex gloves twenty-four hours a day. The other twelve members of the household staff wore fresh white cotton in his presence. Each would receive a new pair for his or her birthday. After thirty years of service, Edgar was awarded a pair of leather gloves near in quality to Bryce's own.

Fortunately for Bryce, the blessed fulcrum of modern technology diminished the need for human contact, once again reinforcing in his mind the interrelationship between progress and isolation. Email, video conferencing, and overnight delivery services allowed him to conduct his business from the comfort of his windowless home office. As the years seeped past, Bryce retreated more and more into his impenetrable shell of seclusion. He was usually visible, especially to crowds and television cameras, but always on the periphery, where he could wave, smile and quickly escape.

Now, safely ensconced behind tinted windows, Bryce inspected his unwitting downtown populace in action. He smiled at the guitar strumming wino with his case open in a futile plea for spare change. He grinned at the overweight mother of two, dragging her young charges along in her wake, yanking their spindly arms so vigorously that their tiny sneakered feet rose above the security of the pavement. He chuckled gleefully at the young couple arguing loudly by their rust-covered Hyundai, threading profanities around unintelligible street phrases regarding something about witnesses, prison time and bills to pay. He even admired the bold strut of the four young men with vivid red hoodies, back-turned baseball caps, or kerchiefs tied around their heads.

He was having a delightful time, until Edgar interrupted his reverie. "I think we should go now, sir," came the almost apologetic voice over the limousine's intercom.

Bryce was about to shout down the chauffeur's impudence, when he was interrupted by a woman's scream. The young couple had moved their discussion to the difficult-to-refute debate tactic known as domestic violence. The boy, for he could be no more than sixteen, was repeatedly striking at his girlfriend's face. She swung wildly at him in return, her blows missing by mere inches.

"Do you see that, Edgar?!" Bryce cried into the phone.

"Yes sir. We really should be leaving."

"Nonsense! Where is your sense of civic duty! That boy just pummeled that woman!"

"Yes, sir. However, it might be wise to let the police handle this."

"There are no police in sight. I want you to go out there and put a stop to this."

"Sir?"

"Break them up. Reason with them. Right this minute! Go ahead!"

Through the glass partition that separated them, Bryce could see the back of Edgar's gray head shaking slowly. There was a pause, before his voice filtered up from the telephone receiver.

"Mr. Townsend...I grew up in this neighborhood. Believe me, it is never...wise...to interfere in an argument like that."

Bryce was furious. These were his people, and he felt an overwhelming responsibility to them. In all the years he had known Edgar, he had never experienced this strain of cowardice in his personal chauffeur. Clearly the man was past his prime, and a new driver would have to be procured just as soon as they arrived back at the estate.

Outside, the woman's screams suddenly rose in volume. Others along the street pretended not to notice, their stares fixed on whatever direction their feet happened to be moving at the time, as if averted eyes could will their ears not to hear her plaintive moans. A few teens recorded the attack on their phones, but made no effort to help.

Bryce could take it no more. He jerked at the receiver and barked into it.

"Edgar! Get out this instant and put a stop to that!!"

After another moment's hesitation, Edgar slowly opened the limousine door. He moved to the front of the long black vehicle, slowly working his way across the searing pavement to the battling couple.

He never made it half that far.

As soon as he was five feet from the car, the young man dropped his girlfriend to the pavement, and in one well-rehearsed move, pulled a silver automatic from his jacket and aimed it at the aging chauffeur. Taking their cue, the four teens in gang colors sprang to action. Two collapsed Edgar to the ground with savage swings of a tire iron, one knocked the cellular telephone antennae off the trunk hood with a baseball bat, while the fourth teen raced to the open front door of the limousine. He scrambled into the driver's seat and slammed the long car in gear. As the limo screeched from the curb, the rest of the gang piled into the suddenly unlocked doors and muscled their way directly into Bryce Townsend IV's private little world.

It all happened so quickly, all the stunned billionaire could think about was how distasteful the inevitable physical contact would be.

****

The merciful blanket of unconsciousness abruptly ripped from his mind, and took with it the numbness that had enveloped him since the savage attack ended. His first returning sense was smell, as his nose was accosted with a foul, acrid stench that rose from his own body. Next was the sense of touch, as every nerve he owned screamed with the shrill, unwanted persistency of an angry alarm clock. He felt himself bleeding, the warm trickle spreading across his face, his eyes, his mouth. He could taste his own blood, and with it came the sudden realization that he was still alive. He could hear the squeal and roar of tires, the whisper of voices, and his own frantically thumping heart.

With great effort, he shoved open his eyelids and squinted up at the cruel shards of intruding sunlight. He found himself splayed on his back in a crumbling gutter, a broken whiskey bottle cutting into his side. His face inches away from a pool of blood-tinted vomit, which may or may not have been his own.

How could this have happened? he wondered through the pain.

How could his people do these vile things to each other?

And how could they even think of doing this to him?

As his eyes gradually meandered into focus, he began to notice the small, impromptu mob hovering above him. They looked deeply concerned, he could see it etched in each lined and weathered face. They must have recognized him at last...knew who he was, and remembered all he had done for them.

His people were here to save him at last.

In reality, what they recognized were the eighteen-hundred dollar Italian silk suits and the four hundred dollar Bruno Maggli imported shoes.

He tried valiantly to smile up at them.

His people took this as a sign. Without a word, they stripped him to his underwear, then left him, surprised and frightened, in the unforgiving gutter.

****

He woke again hours later with a start, \ feeling the unwelcome groping of a stranger's hands. As one of his eyelids pushed open, a pair of large black eyes stared down at him, peering with invasive curiosity. Frightened and repulsed, he propelled himself forward and gripped at the hovering shoulders with stiffened fingers.

"Back off, buddy!" The woman barked at him. "I'm a nun. If God don't smite you for those roaming hands, I sure as hell will!"

She shoved him back to the table with what he believed was more force than necessary, but what she deemed was just right. His mind started to push through the retreating tide of disorientation. Eventually, he discovered himself to be lying on a rickety steel table in a run-down examining room, that appeared to pay homage to the design firm of Kitsch, Bankruptcy and Disease.

"Wha...?" was all he could mutter through his badly swollen lips and jaw.

She looked deep into his face again and softened slightly, which is to say, not at all.

"Good question. You're at the Saint Agnes of Mercy Clinic in the Bronx. You are the victim of an accident or an assault...beaten like a bad soufflé, by the looks of it."

"...who...?"

"Another good question. I'm Sister Josette. Ministering to the sick, the lost and the morally bankrupt." She eyed him with thinly disguised repulsion. "Congratulations. Judging by the smell of cheap wine and vomit on you, I'd say you qualify for all three."

"My...limo..."

"Your limo? That's one I don't hear very often. Don't worry. Your limo is parked out back next to my Rolls Royce and Mother Superior's Jaguar. Sister Bernadette is polishing the chrome now. You did want the hot wax treatment, didn't you?"

Bryce Townsend IV looked up to the strange woman, and tried to comprehend what she was saying. He studied the crinkles around her large, doe-like eyes, the smooth line of her cheek, the ringlets of glistening black hair that framed her generous face, and realized that she was quite beautiful. Then he realized the meaning of her words.

"...sarcasm..."

"Think so?" she smiled broadly, a glistening line of teeth, perfectly crafted for smiling. "It is one of the harmless vices I allow myself. It helps keep me sane, while I mingle with the dregs of society's wine barrel. Nothing personal, you understand." She smiled again, and he felt levitated by the crystalline joy she exuded.

Then, the pain hit him like an overdue bank loan. Every inch of his body suddenly screamed in an abrupt onslaught of agony. He began to convulse, and would have shrieked, if his face and throat didn't hurt so much.

Seeing his suffering, Josette's bemused expression immediately shifted to one of concern and professionalism. Bryce never felt the shot, but the injection of morphine brought him a slow, lumbering wave of comfort that gradually pushed back against the pain. The shaking stopped and a feeling of peace eased the contortions of his disfigured face. The shattered and wired jaw, fiercely swollen, turned his encroaching smile into a hideous grimace, but the young nun recognized it just the same.

"Sleep well, you poor. unlucky soul," she whispered, as he gratefully receded from consciousness. "God is on your side, and lucky for you, I play back-up on his team."

✳✳

For twenty-three consecutive days, Sister Josette ministered to the pitiful man with the disfigured face. He had been savagely beaten, worse than anyone she had seen in weeks, and there was a chance he might not recover. On those few days he regained consciousness, he managed only to choke out fragments of barely audible nonsense involving huge estates and philanthropy betrayed. This was not unusual in cases this severe. In the past two years alone, she had nursed back to comparative health two Napoleons, a Queen Elizabeth and a half-dozen Jesus Christs. She patched them up, put them back on the street, then patched them up once more when the drugs, the violence and the ferocity of their lifestyles returned them, time and again, to her overburdened clinic. It was a gnawing cycle of human destruction of which she was merely a well-intentioned cohort. For many in this most wretched part of town, her gruff, but consistent presence was the only obstacle standing between a miserable life and a tragic death.

Yet, despite her charitable actions, the young nun was filled with the most unholy of thoughts. These were God's people, she knew, so she ministered to them as she believed she must. But in her heart, she hated the very people she was saving. She hated their choices, their voluntary participation in their own self destruction. She saw herself as aiding the decline of the greater society by perpetuating the vicious. The prostitute with AIDS who laughed at the unwitting customers she infected each day. The savage gang members who preyed on the weak and elderly, but came to her whenever they got themselves shot or stabbed. The psychopathic drifters who moved from town to town, always one step ahead of the police, racking up a body count she dared not think about. Day after day she ministered to them, healed them, comforted them, encouraged them, and even prayed for them. And most of all, she hated herself for hating them. God must have a reason for creating souls such as these, she thought darkly, but she could only pray it was a damn good reason.

Each morning and evening, Sister Josette held the hand of the man with the disfigured face and wired jaw, as she read to him passages from the Bible, War and Peace, and a half-dozen poorly written books by some crazy billionaire, which someone had donated to the clinic. At first, he pulled his hand back, as if terrified by her touch. However, as the days and weeks slipped past, his grip relaxed, until he seemed almost comfortable in her grasp.

She wondered who he was, how he had ended up in that gutter with no clothes, no identification, a severe swelling in his throat had cut off his voice the day after he had arrived, and left him desperately grunting in a cruel mockery of the art of communication. She imagined a history for him, not dissimilar to the millions of hard luck stories she had heard during her long years in the slums. He was an alcoholic who probably abused his children, abandoned his wife when she was pregnant with her eighth child, and was running from the police when he was foolish enough to stumble into the worst neighborhood in the city. Even though she despised him for the pain she was sure he must have inflicted on good people all his life, she spent hours each day by his side, tending his wounds, stroking his hair, and washing the tears from his still swollen face. Tears, not of pain, but of a suffering even more profound. She could not decipher the war raging inside her patient, so she soothed it away with soft words and an occasional kiss on the forehead.

She dubbed him "The Wretch," which she was secretly pleased to see annoyed him immensely, even though his crushed larynx prevented him from objecting in more than unintelligible grunts. She knew that, if he lived, his face would likely remain permanently disfigured from the brutal assault, and she surprised herself by crying over that fact. The young nun had seen so much suffering and so much evil in this place, she was afraid she had lost the capacity to be emotionally touched by these poor souls who constantly begged for help. To survive in a sea of misery, she reasoned, one must become numb to it, and so she permitted a great callous to grow around her heart.

"I'll heal you. I'll feed you, and I'll even pray for you," Sister Josette often grumbled at her charges, "But don't ever expect me to like you."

Yet, The Wretch was different. There was a hunger in the way he held her hand. Not savage, not sexual, or even frightened. It was...unusual. As if he lived for her touch, drew strength from it. She could tell by the way his fingers melted into hers. She somehow felt she could really reach this one.

But she always felt she could reach them.

She should know better, she told herself.

One morning, while she was at Mass, the police came and took The Wretch away. There had been some sort of commotion, which Franky the heroin addict tried to explain to her, but the malnourished junky had long ago lost the ability to connect two logical thoughts, or communicate a simple sentence to anyone.

"They got 'em. Should'a seen it! Got 'em. Man, like it was... They got 'em, Sister!" Franky shouted to the worried nun. "He's was like...y'know, The Wretch, I mean, somebody. Really somebody, I mean! Really, and they got 'em, friggin' cops..."

After more than fifteen minutes of this, Sister Josette finally gave up trying to find out exactly what happened to The Wretch, or why the police took him away. After all, she had a hundred cases just as pitiful demanding her attention.

As she strolled down the cramped hallway, she tried to forget the one patient who had almost touched her heart.

She was dismayed to see how easy it was.

****

"Are you Sister Josette?" the well-dressed chauffeur asked her. She noticed the middle-aged black man was accompanied by two burly thugs in gray suits, who, judging by their carelessly concealed shoulder holsters, were obviously well-armed.

At least they weren't stupid enough to come into this kind of neighborhood unprepared.

"Actually, I'm Beyonce. I just come to this clinic to get away from my adoring fans."

Edgar looked at the woman with curiosity. It had been seven months since the attack that nearly ended his life, and this was the first and last time he ever planned to return to this God-forsaken slum. Now, on top of everything, he had to deal with a sarcastic nun.

"I really need to know if you are Sister Josette...uh, Sister." His eyes flitted nervously over the dozens of grimy faces that glared at him from dingy hallways. Instinctively, he drew closer to the bodyguards on both sides of him.

"Yes, okay," she uttered with genuine exhaustion. "I'm Sister Josette, patron saint of the city's unwashed. What can I do for you? Whatever it is, make it snappy. I got a fourteen year-old in the other room who may be bleeding to death from a botched abortion. Her third I might add."

Edgar looked at the nun with a strange blend of contempt and admiration. He wondered how she could be foolish enough to give so much of herself to these people. People who would eagerly cut her throat for the small gold cross hanging from her neck. He wanted to ask her why, but he was suddenly overcome by a desperate need to return to the safety of his new, armor-plated limousine.

"This is for you," he said, as he shoved a book into her hand. Then, without another word, Edgar the chauffeur turned quickly and half-trotted out the door to the haven of his waiting vehicle. The two bodyguards followed him outside, eyeballed the street for a long moment, then disappeared inside the steel-reinforced doors, as the limousine screeched from the curb and eventually retreated to a less threatening world.

Sister Josette looked down at the book in her hands. It was another diatribe by that crazy billionaire, like those she would read to her most severe cases. Only this book seemed far less optimistic than the others.

"The Collapse Of Civilization," the title shouted in blood red letters.

The weary nun shook her head and tossed the book to Franky the heroin addict, who was back at the clinic with his seventeenth needle infection this year.

"Here, Franky," she smiled. "Come read how the other half lives."

She was halfway down the packed corridor, when Franky came scurrying up behind her. He seemed more excited than even his hot-wired brain was accustomed to being.

"Sister Josette...Sister, This, I mean. This was, um, in the, you know, that book. Really!" He handed her an expensive looking linen envelope.

Sister Josette examined the white envelope with her name carefully inscribed in fine calligraphy. She tore it open and removed a piece of equally expensive stationary. The handwriting was scrawled, as if by someone with limited use of his hands, the result of a stroke, perhaps.

She read the letter out loud.

"You have touched my life more than you know. This is for you, with one unbreakable condition... You must promise never to spend a penny of it on anyone but yourself."

She smirked at that. Then her eyes fell to the signature on the bottom of the letter.

It read simply, The Wretch.

She pulled a second piece of paper from the envelope and her eyes widened. It was a check written from the account of the Bryce Townsend IV Philanthropic Fund. The check was written in the amount of ten million dollars.

Sister Josette smiled, shook her long curls from her eyes, then casually handed the check to Franky.

His face contorted in more directions at once than the nun would have thought humanly possible.

"This..." he sputtered. "This is like...like ten million!"

"Yeah," she sighed. "Pretty funny joke, huh? I didn't even know The Wretch had a sense of humor." Her smile slowly faded, as she remembered the desperate yearning feel of his hand in hers.

"What... Whatcha gonna do with it? All that money, I mean?" Franky held the check like it was on fire.

"You take it, Franky. Maybe you can get enough for a fix before it bounces through the roof."

"But...but it's made out to you, Sister?!"

"So, forge my name." She shrugged. "You do it on those stolen morphine prescriptions all the time." She leaned forward and wiped a stream of tears from the face of a small Hispanic boy in the hallway. "Besides, it's gotta be fake." She bent down to kiss the head of the six year-old child. "We all know there's no such thing as philanthropy in this part of town."

Sister Josette scooped up the frightened child in her arms, and gently carried him into a dingy examining room.

The cracked wooden door closed slowly behind her, as Franky the heroin addict eagerly stuffed the check in his pocket and scuttled off in search of a pen.

Second Week

It finally hit him.

Hit him like a kick in the ribs, forcing his breath to die in his throat.

It wasn't lying alone each night in the cold, empty bed.

It wasn't the day he pulled the cheap chest of drawers up the narrow, rickety stairs by himself, straining his weeping heart far more than his back.

It wasn't the last load of laundry he did in that house before he could find a cheap Laundromat, or the extra hours that were somehow cruelly added to each long sleepless night, staring at the frustratingly regular rotation of the ceiling fan.

It hit him with a simple sentence related by a friend; a friend who had called his house, his former house, and then called his cell phone in a panic.

A friend who told him what his wife, his former wife, had said, with a toneless simplicity in her voice.

"He doesn't live here anymore," she had said.

And that's when it finally hit him.

After a week spirited away in a grimy motel room with only the coarse chatter of unfamiliar voices outside his first-floor window to keep him company, he stole away to a hiding place of a different sort, a small room in the home of a friend's mother. An eighty year-old former circus performer who regaled him with stories of past adventures every time she saw the look in his eye grow slowly numb. She spoke of clowns and con men and carnies and elephants and wondrous emotions he had long ago misplaced. And he watched her face soften with the tales of her own husband, who she never called by name, but always referred to simply as 'her husband.' And as she mouthed the words with such faraway tenderness, her distant expression relaxed into a smile that betrayed a love that could not die, even though the object of her affections had, after only seven brief years of marriage. Yet in those seven years, she had loved a lifetime, with a devotion that still leaked from her eyes and entwined her heart some fifty years later.

As she spun her rich remembrances of romance won and lost, he softly wondered whether he would himself ever be a part of anyone's history, not fifty years from now, that was too much to hope for, but even next month, for he felt his hold on the world eroding, and his place in it already swept away. He retreated to his temporary room, unpacked suitcases, and the silently condemning ceiling fan, and feared he was no longer part of anyone's history, not even his own.

And as his second week beyond marriage slunk by, he continued to refuse the kind and concerned offers of friends and family who wanted to talk, each secretly fearing he would cave in on himself if he held it in much longer. He understood their good intentions, appreciated their concern. For he had seen so many other relationships scream or moan to a close, and had often leant an ear of sympathy to those in pain. But in this case, he would rather listen, than be listened to. Despite their jealous insistence, he refused with a grateful smile, for inner collapse was exactly what he yearned for now. That promise of emotional implosion was all that sustained him in this strange, tiny room in somebody else's house, lost within a life that was so obviously not his own.

"You have to talk about it," they insisted. "You can't keep everything bottled up inside." But in truth, he was less worried about things bottled up inside, than letting them know his deepest fear.

That there might be nothing left inside him at all.

He knew that some would see his silence as proof of the bitter accusations his ex-wife was spreading about him. Tales of illicit affairs and wild parties he must be throwing to celebrate his long-plotted wreckage of their marriage. She told everyone that he must surely be wallowing in the depravity of his newfound single status. And he knew that as each day went by without denials or counter-charges, these stories would grow shriller, with increasing absurdity and blame.

So it had been with the unraveling of her first marriage, for some choose to play divorce as a game, and the one who ends up with the most sympathetic friends wins. Yet he had chosen not to play that game, not out of nobility or lack of talent, for he had often matched her accusation for accusation before.

But this time it was different.

He had no heart for destroying her.

Because deep down, he felt he already had.

Even though he realized embellished fears and lurid lies would gradually be seen as truth when repeated often enough, since we all share the ugly trait of first believing the worst about a person, still he chose to remain silent. To keep to himself. Experience had taught him that each retelling of a harsh tale, even to a sympathetic ear, would close another path to reconciliation. For how could others empathetically absorb the biased perspectives and personal attacks, exaggerated into fiction by vengefulness and hurt, then be expected to forget, if the injured parties were ever to come back together? Life is seldom clean, and wounds left exposed are less likely to heal. Once you force someone outside a relationship to choose sides, something inside them always will, even when the battles are over and grudging truces are declared.

He also knew from experience that each bitter story also takes its toll on the teller, until every lie becomes more real to a defensively hardened heart.

And so, the man who had spent so much of his life enslaved to the opinions of others, grew suddenly dispassionate as to what anyone might think about this single most tragic turn in his life.

Instead, he buried himself in work and worry. Attended movies alone, and twice embraced the embarrassed solitude of a table for one, knowing that those around him knew he was there not by choice, but by failure of heart or personality. As he choked down food without flavor or enjoyment, he muttered silent prayers that no one he knew would see him so exposed, so publicly flayed. He prayed to be invisible from the world, from his past, from himself.

When he was forced to speak, he spoke of anything but the separation, even while he spent endless hours thinking of nothing else.

Despite the increasingly shrill rumors, which swirled around him like silent, all-consuming locusts, he saw no one outside of work, and gradually, the outside became less and less real to him. Soon, even his innermost thoughts took on a curiously dreamlike quality. He felt no more a part of himself than his clothing, which had become increasingly unkempt and repetitious, and he suddenly wondered if anyone had noticed he had worn the same rumpled green shirt and mismatched black socks for days on end.

In desperation, he tried to escape into a novel of absurd thickness, which he cursed himself for completing before the week was out. He hoped this dense tale of India two centuries ago, with its colorful promise of empires, heroism, and war could distract him from the non-exotic existence of just another soon-to-be-divorced, middle-aged man alone in a rented room. Yet, the book entranced him for too brief a time, as he tried to soothe himself with tales of epic suffering and selfless nobility. The tears would come at the most curious points; whenever a character, scarred from battle and long past the point of hope, would happen upon a kindness of fate, or inexplicably comforted by caring arms and the sweet voices of welcome. Slowly, his body would shake with soundless sobs, because he did not want to disturb the kindly circus lady with his own failings and foolishness.

One morning, he found himself no longer sure he could survive this. He assured himself, he was never in danger of self-mutilation, at least in the physical sense. Yet, if he could have found a pre-dug grave to hide within, he would have gladly accepted its moldy embrace. Even as he gracefully sidestepped the sympathetic prattle of others, he both envied and despised those for whom divorce had become a necessary habit, or merely an inconvenience to be endured every few years.

Though it was cruel, even to himself, he kept a picture of her, the woman who was no longer his, resting on the small desk facing his twin bed. His favorite image of two young lovers captured on a honeymoon in Jamaica, their eyes shimmering with surprised joy, their arms entwined with the comfortable familiarity of those to whom touch was simply another language of affection. He looked at the picture now and admired her beauty once more. But he also sensed she had become a stranger to him, as had the younger picture of himself with the comfortable, contended expression. These people were no more part of him now than the creatures of fiction in the novel of India that had also ended much too soon. Yet, as he looked into their time-frozen faces, he envied their removal from the ravages of reality, as if that single moment they lived in that snapshot was infinitely preferable to the long, grinding years, in which their lifelong affection succumbed to the onslaught of a million and four petty arguments.

He was sure he didn't love her anymore, and was shocked to discover that he suddenly didn't love or like or care about anyone or anything at all. He had become a withered and battered vessel, broken from its mooring by a vicious squall, with nothing substantial to hold it to land or function, drifting aimlessly off into increasingly dark and empty waters.

This terrified him most of all.

The seductive numbness.

The slow surrender of all attachments.

He was becoming a ghost in his own life. A water stain on the ceiling, familiar, always present, but routinely ignored. He found himself choking on the perverse, claustrophobic freedom of anonymity.

Belonging to nothing. To no one.

With nothing to say. And even less to prove.

A wisp of smoke where a man had once been.

A walking void, with no history, no emotions, no purpose.

Each day, there was little left inside him. Not even regret.

So this is what separation feels like? he muttered beneath the whirr of the overly judgmental ceiling fan.

And ten minutes later, the silent sobs returned once more.

THE ENCOUNTER

"Damn it, Harlan! We gotta be there in twenty minutes!"

Harlan Jessup didn't need to see the pockmarked face, or the substantial beer belly hanging over the old leather belt like some slow avalanche of excess; he knew the voice that barged in from the outer office, had known it since his earliest days at Stonewall Jackson Elementary.

The intrusive voice belonged to his best friend, Gil Bledsoe.

And, as usual, Gil was pissed.

"You hear me, Harlan?!"

"Don't bust a blood vessel, Gil. I'll be done and out in two!" Harlan hollered in reply. With a heavy sigh, he examined his face in the cold reflection of his bathroom mirror. He was getting too old for this. Getting too old for everything.

"Damn it all, Harlan! Hurry your ass up! I don't wanna be missin' the whole parade!" Gil shouted from the lobby.

Muttering a string of silent obscenities, Harlan splashed cold water on his face, splashed it again, and then a third time, feeling absolved by the icy sting on his freshly-shaven jowls.

Why he felt he always had to shave for these things, he had no idea.

"I said I don't wanna be missin' this parade, Harlan!!"

"And I said I'll be done and out in two!" Harlan's voice echoed in the cramped office bathroom. "So control your damn butt muscles, Gil!!"

He was definitely getting too old for this. They all were.

Harlan watched himself drag a frayed brown towel over the drooping contours of his face. He took stock of the recent sag of skin beneath his furry brows that betrayed his age, the spidery map of alcohol-ruptured blood vessels that betrayed his weekend hobby, and the haunted cast of his dulled eyes that betrayed his past. Disgusted by this mocking inventory, Harlan Jessup sighed and stepped into his small, paneled office.

"Come on, Harlan! Ain't you ready yet?"

"Just go and turn on the ball game, Gil! I'll be out when I'm good and goddam ready!"

"Is that 'Bama playin'?"

"Channel Eight." Harlan shook his head, then muttered to himself, "Never seen a man so all-fired anxious to dress up like the Pillsbury Doughboy..." And with that, he tugged heavily on the rough corded sash that affixed his white ceremonial robe, branding him as a member in good standing of the Huntsville chapter of the Grand Order of the Knights of the Klu Klux Klan.

The sparsely furnished office resembled a shrine to diminished dreams and atrophied ambition. On the far wall, a once-proud banner boasted the words: JESSUP INSURANCE AGENCY, now humbled by age and overuse. It drooped off the cracked paneling, flanked by two free-standing flags -- one American, one Confederate. In front of the frayed banner, a battered, cigarette scored pine desk, a vintage COMPAQ computer that hadn't worked in years, a cheap Chinese laptop that didn't work much better, and a gangly stack of scattered manila folders that threatened to topple over with the slightest breeze and groan from the rickety, dust-filled ceiling fan.

The one shred of luxury was a high-backed executive chair given to Harlan by the Grand Wizard himself, in appreciation for saving the chapter a great deal of money on health and term life insurance. The executive chair was amply padded and covered with a rose tweed upholstery material. It was the pride of Harlan's office, and his cocoon when he needed to escape from friends like Gil.

"Nice outfit," said the girl in the Straight Outta Compton t-shirt and tight jeans. She smiled as she saw the overweight Klansman stagger back in surprise. "Who's your tailor? Casper, the friendly ghost?"

"Damn! You half-scared the heart right outa me!"

"I know," she smirked from her perch in Harlan's prized executive chair. "You're white as a sheet."

"Who the hell are you?" the older man panted, as he struggled to regain his composure. He knew he must look like an idiot, hopping backwards, dressed in his oversized Klan sheet. "And how'd the hell'd you get in here?!"

Harlan studied the smirking woman behind his desk. A teenager, he guessed. Disturbingly pretty. And black. A young black girl in his office. In his chair. He could feel the rush of blood in his face, as he barked out...

"And what the hell are you doing in my office?!"

"I came to see you," she shrugged, with no discernible interest.

"What for?"

"Not fashion advice, that's for damn sure."

His eyes narrowed into a wicked squint. This smart-mouthed kid was taunting him, disrespecting him in his own office. "This here's private property, little girl. You know I could shoot you down for just bein' here?"

"And get nigger blood all over this pretty padded chair?" She took the measure of him in turn, and refused to cringe. "Now that would be a real shame."

"You got a smart mouth. You know that, girly?"

"Yes, sir. I get it from my mother."

"A smart mouth can get you in real trouble 'round here."

"I know that, too. My momma got in real trouble once. And nine months later, there I was."

He took a few heavy steps toward the desk, and sized up the situation. Even though she was sitting down, he guessed he was a full head taller than her, and outweighed her by seventy or ninety pounds at least. Judging by what she was wearing, it was clear she wasn't carrying any type of weapon. That last observation put Harlan at ease. "You think you're funny, don't ya, girl?"

"My teachers always said I had a noticeable ability to amuse myself."

The young woman rose out of the chair and casually scanned the room. She paid particular attention to the photos of Harlan and his friends along the walls. She appeared completely comfortable here, as if she were examining exhibits in a school science fair. By contrast, Harlan, still caught in his white sheet, seemed far more nervous.

"Look, girly-girl, I don't know what game your playin'. But I don't think you know what you're dealin' with here."

She spun around with such sudden fury, the big man was forced to take a step backward.

"First of all, the name is Tricia! Tricia Hardwick. Not girly-girl. Got it?!" She kept her voice low in volume, though it was bursting with rage and contempt. "And second of all, I know exactly what I'm dealing with here... Some low-rent cracker so afraid of us black folk, he gotta hide behind a bedsheet and an army of brain-dead, whisky-sucking rednecks, who burp for a living, cheat on their wives, and try to convince each other they're really the superior race!"

They glared at each other, feeling the tension grab each by the throat and shove them toward disaster. Strangely enough, it was Harlan's expression that softened first.

"Okay...so you do know what you're dealing with," he snorted with amusement, then added, "The next question is, what do you want?"

"Like I said. I came to see you," Tricia replied, not sharing his amusement.

They were still on the brink; him in his Klan outfit, her in a t-shirt that screamed black defiance, and with Gil, the back-up racist, waiting in the outer lobby. Tricia suspected, while Harlan knew, that any moment, the introduction of Gil in the room could make this tenuous situation explode.

Harlan spread his thick hands and put on his friendliest voice. "Look, Trixie or Tanisha, or whatever the hell your name is…if you're lookin' for insurance, these ain't my regular workin' hours. Why don't you just come on back when the office is open?"

Now it was Tricia's turn to stiffen. She walked right past him and directed her words to the Confederate flag.

"I came to tell you she's dead," she said softly.

"Who's dead?"

"Lydia."

Harlan's left fist clenched. The stubby fingers of his right flexed twice. He turned away from her and studied a small scratch on the desktop that may or may not have been dust.

"Lydia who?" he whispered, immediately hating the quaver in his voice.

"Lydia Hardwick, you son of a bitch!" She had no hope of restraining her anger. "And don't you try to tell me you don't know who I'm talking about. After what you and your kind did to her!"

Harlan crossed to the far window, avoiding her gaze. He didn't have to answer. Didn't have to explain. Not to this girl. Not to anybody. He could even deny the whole thing; after all, it was half a lifetime ago, but somehow, he knew it would be useless.

"How'd she die?" he asked, so quietly, she could barely hear the words.

"Figure it out."

He nodded, "She always did have a bad heart." His eyes were fixed on a scene of panic and terror framed by memory, not the grimy window he stared through now.

"No, Mister Jessup. She always had a good heart. A wonderful heart..." He could hear the sorrow that ransacked her voice. "It just never beat quite like everybody else's."

The big man turned back to the girl in time to catch her wiping the tear from her cheek. "You're kin to her, I'm guessin'?"

"Her daughter. She never had none but me."

"What about her husband? He with her when she passed?"

"She didn't 'pass' Mr. Jessup," her words tainted with accusation. "She died. She died alone. While I was at college." And then she added softly. "And to answer your question, she never did marry."

"So that makes you some kind of bastard, huh?"

"That makes us both bastards, Mister Jessup...I'm nineteen. Do the math yourself."

He did.

"Aww...Christ..."

"The Lord had nothing whatsoever to do with this."

This time the thick silence was punctured by Gil's bellow. "What the hell you doin' in there, Harlan? You got the TV on or somethin'? Don't you know we got us some niggers to terrorize?"

Tricia's eyes squeezed out hatred that lasered deep into Harlan's chest.

"Say one more word, Gil," he hollered to the outer lobby as he locked eyes with Lydia's daughter. "One more thing and I'm gonna put a bullet in that thick skull of yours! You hear me?!"

A pause.

Then the whiny reply...

"I just don't wanna be late... I don't see why it takes you so all-fired long to..."

"I'm getting my gun, Gil!"

Neither moved through the silence that followed, neither did they flinch or look away, until Gil's chastened voice crept back through the door.

"You got any beer, at least?"

Harlan smiled, as he yelled to the outer office, "In the fridge. There's some Hamm's in the fridge." Then he turned back to Tricia. "So... what exactly is it you want with me?"

"Nothing. I'm just here to tell you the news, is all."

"Bullshit. You may think I'm some dumb heap of white trash, but even I don't buy that."

"Fair enough...I don't know. I had to see you, I guess." She had to whisper to keep from crying. "Had to see the man who raped my momma."

Harlan turned from her, drawn to the window once more. "He ain't in this room, little girl."

"You raped my momma, Mr. Jessup! You raped my momma and left me as some walking-talking trophy of your pitiful white aggression!"

He spoke so softly, and with such careful, profound distress, that Tricia would have thought it impossible a sound so small could emerge from such a large figure.

"Is that what she told you?" he mumbled.

"No. Momma never said nothing about you. But I could see the pain in her eyes. Lord, that woman hurt more than one human being has a right to."

Harlan nodded. "Then who told you I raped your momma? Your uncles?"

"At her funeral. I had to know. They told me how you raped her when she was only seventeen, then left her bleeding and begging for mercy in the tobacco field."

Harlan closed his eyes and saw her now; Lydia.

Lydia Hardwick....

He heard her cries.

Smelled the damp tobacco leaves whipping his skin as he ran...

"Well, they got it half right, anyways," he mumbled, as much to himself as her.

"You trying to deny it?" she stomped over to his corner of the room. "You trying to tell me you're not my daddy?!"

He abandoned the window. Turned to face her again.

"Look, little girl..."

"Tricia! My name is Tricia! At least you can learn that much about me, you bastard!" Her fists were clenched, and Harlan knew she was one lie away from striking him. He just couldn't be sure what he would do, if she tried.

"Look, Tricia." he cringed. "I... I knew your momma."

"Nice way to phrase it."

"Okay, let me say it better..." The hulking Klansman towered over the young girl, who shrank under his sudden onslaught. "I loved your momma. Does that make you feel any better?! Huh?!"

His words slapped her into silence.

"That's right! You wanna hear me say it again? I loved Lydia. Loved her more than anybody I ever met in my whole, damn, useless life!"

"If you loved her so damn much, why did you...?!"

Harlan grabbed her thin arms and shoved her toward the desk.

"What are y...?"

"Just sit down and shut up, okay?! If you're gonna make me tell you this, I'm gonna see you're at least respectful enough to listen!"

"You can't talk to me like that!"

"I can do what the hell I please! I'm your goddamn daddy, remember?!"

Harlan shoved the defiant teen into the chair. He towered over her, his meaty hands holding her firmly in place. Trixie looked up at him with a volatile mix of panic and hatred, as if she suddenly realized how dangerous her position truly was.

For his part, Tricia's fearful expression was eerily similar to her mother's, and that thought hit Harlan like a battering ram. He released his fingers, shrunk away from those searing eyes, and the pain they rekindled in his memory. When he finally met her stare again, he was a different man, softer, more deferential.

"Just sit...please. I ain't talked this out loud in near on twenty years... Old wounds ain't pretty when they open up again." His head drooped with the weight of too many memories. "Best not to stand too close."

She was surprised by his sudden change in mood. He was too threatening, too unpredictable.

"I'm listening," she said, crossing her arms.

He retreated to his position by the window, and she had to strain to hear his words.

"Lydia...your momma... She was everything to me. Beautiful...like you. Smart mouthed, like you. Full of life, y'know? I was on the football team at Southland. You might not guess that to look at me now..."

"Let me guess. Tackling dummy?"

"Wide receiver."

"I can understand the 'wide' part."

He couldn't help but smile, recognizing the wild and sarcastic spark of Lydia in her.

"Your momma, she kept to herself mostly. But I loved her the first time I caught that strange look in her eyes..." He turned to her now. "You say you saw pain in her eyes, and maybe that's so. But I saw only life. Sweet, sweet life and laughter, oozin' outa her like nobody else in the world had claim to it. She made me feel..."

Again, he returned to the safety of the window, his back to her once more.

"Hell, let's just say I loved her and leave it at that. I didn't give a damn what anybody thought. The hell with my friends. The hell with 'em all. All I cared about was marrying Lydia Hardwick and losing myself in her eyes forever."

"You saying you didn't rape her?"

"No. I didn't rape her. But we were stupid. We were carryin' on in secret and she got pregnant. What could I do? I couldn't tell my family, they'd never understand. Hell, my daddy woulda shot me for fraternizin' with a Negro. So I figured we'd run off together. New Orleans or something. It didn't matter where. Not to me. And not to her."

Tricia looked across the room at the redneck in the white Klan robe, a man who represented everything she had grown to despise. Yet for some strange reason, she did not, she could not, doubt the sincerity in his voice.

"But you never made it to New Orleans?" she whispered.

"No. We never made it...Lydia, she was so pig-headed. But in a lovable way, y'know?"

Now it was her turn to turn away.

"Yeah. I know."

"She couldn't just sneak off, like I begged her to. That wasn't her. We were already on the road, when she stopped dead and wouldn't walk another step. She just had to tell her Daddy good-bye."

He closed his eyes and saw her again, the adorable, immovable set of her jaw when she made up her mind about something. He gently shook the image from his head. "I tried to talk her out of it, of course. Told her what would happen if people found out about us. But you know your momma."

Tricia sat, decades away from him, and nodded silently.

"When we went back, her brothers were there. And just like I warned her, they started a big old fight."

Tricia saw the thick muscles tighten on his neck, noticed how his large, whitened fingers began to twist at the rope sash around his waist. His gravel-edged voice grew more serrated as he continued.

"Your uncles... They weren't gonna let their little sis marry no white boy. They blamed me for what a handful of people I ain't ever met did a hundred years before my kin even came to this country! Like it was my fault, and always will be! I told them I was gonna marry her. Protect her. Do it up right. But they wouldn't have none of that. So, I grabbed her then and there, and we took off runnin' across the tobacco fields. When she couldn't run no more, 'cuz she was pregnant and all, I carried her. There we were, runnin' like crazy with her in my arms like a baby. A love-sick wide receiver runnin' for his life."

He closed his eyes and found himself back in that tobacco field; Lydia's frightened arms around his neck, the tobacco leaves slashing his arms and legs as he ran. Even in the cold, cruel moonlight, her lovely black cheek pressed in warm contrast to his heaving white chest. Their tears the same silvery color.

On and on he ran with her in his arms, the angry men closing in behind them. On he stumbled through the tall tobacco plants, ran for all he was worth, ran for any hope of a future with Lydia. His Lydia. He could feel his muscles sear with exhaustion, the breath exploding from his lungs. And he cringed from the familiar fear that, no matter how strong he was, no matter how fast he ran, he would not be able to hold her long enough.

He winced suddenly, then opened his eyes to the sparse office and a less tangible, less comforting present.

It was a long moment before he could speak again.

"Anyway, your uncles, they caught up to us. And they showed me... convinced me your momma and me wasn't right for each other."

Tricia trembled with confusion and outrage. Why hadn't her momma told her any of this? Why had she hid this late night terror from her child? She felt betrayed and took her anger out on the heavy-set brute by the window. "Just like that, Mr. Jessup? You get my momma pregnant... and my uncles just *convince* you to walk away?!"

"Well, darlin'..." Slowly, Harlan pulled the heavy white robe off his shoulders. "They did a little more than just convincing."

Tricia gasped and recoiled from the vicious remnants of that night in the tobacco field, a thick spider web of red welts crisscrossing his broad back. Almost against her will, she moved closer to the grotesque signature of rage he wore across his shoulders.

"They didn't all happen that night, of course." he mumbled over his shoulder. "I got some from the second and third lessons." He tried in vain to choke back the sobs. "Finally, I couldn't take it no more.... I guess I just got tired of stumblin' down to old Doc Porter's house."

Tricia was surprised at the tears which streamed down her own cheeks. She reached out a tenuous hand to touch the cruel patterns of raised flesh, the terrible scars which, over the last two decades, had worked their way straight through to his soul. Her fingers pulled back quickly as a voice boomed in from the outer office.

"Harlan, if you don't get your fat ass out here right now, I'm gonna come in there and drag it out!"

Harlan turned to face her, the young girl who looked so much like Lydia. His Lydia. But his Lydia in memory only. He raised a pale thick hand to wipe a single tear from her ebony cheek, but he could not. With less than a foot of space between them, each felt a distance too great, too ancient; separated as they were by pigment, memories, missed opportunities and other people's fears and fanaticism.

His trembling hand dropped uncomfortably to his side.

She understood completely.

"You best be going," was all he could mumble.

She nodded, but could not turn away. Her feet felt heavy and she could not lift them. "Mr. Jessup...I..."

He looked to the floor and shook his head viciously. "Don't say it. Please don't say anything." He quickly tugged the robe back onto his shoulders to hide his humiliation. "It was all too many years ago. I'm too old and empty and twisted up inside to live through any of that again."

He hesitated, there was so much more he wanted to say; so much he wanted to know about Lydia, about Lydia and her daughter. Lydia and his child. Instead, he wiped his eyes with the starched white sleeve, grabbed his hood and crossed to the office door.

"You best wait about twenty minutes, then leave out the back. You don't want Gil or any of the boys to catch you anywhere around here." He did not look at her when he said, "No telling what those brain-dead, whisky-suckin' rednecks might do."

Tricia was incredulous. "You mean, you're still gonna march?"

He released a deep, staccato breath, still unable to meet her eyes. "I... I'd rather you don't stop by this way again, y'hear?"

She heard.

She heard and she understood.

"Good-bye, Mr. Jessup..." she whispered, then added almost to herself. "...daddy..."

"Good-bye, Tricia girl." His words ached like an open wound. "Look, if there's anything you need...?"

"Nothing," She said quickly. "I don't need nothing."

Harlan nodded. Slowly, he raised his Klan hood, placed it on his head, and turned to face his daughter.

The young black woman would not allow herself to look away. She stared deep into the shamed and weary eyes behind the mask, before Harlan P. Jessup, insurance salesman and weekend bigot, turned and escaped out the office door, slamming it behind him. Tricia heard Gil's inebriated voice greet his heavy footsteps.

"Well, it's about damn time, Harlan!"

"Shut the hell up, Gil. Let's get outa here."

"It's about damn time, is all I'm sayin'..."

As she listened for the jarring rattle of the screen door, Tricia Hardwick collapsed into her father's prized executive chair, and imagined a love left bleeding in a tobacco field a lifetime ago.

ETERNITY EMBRACED

Distant screams of agony seeped in through the solemn stone walls and anxious barricades of wood and marble furniture. A lifetime of carefully considered accumulation now pressed in a panicked heap against the barred wooden door, its final worth judged by the sheer weight of each piece, not its artistry.

A desperate wail of pain.

Closer.

Ever closer.

Paulus stood immobile by the door, a rock against the tide, his hawk-like brown eyes stealing from the barricade to the quiet preparations of his tearful wife. Even now, Messalina was sure to be judged the most beautiful woman in all of Rome.

Even now.

Her long black hair cascaded in a sparkling procession of ebony curls that teased and caressed her slender waist as lovingly as he so recently had done. She ran a heavy silver brush through those gentle curls, stopping only to dab the errant moisture from her frightened eyes with a small square of vermilion cloth. There was a defiant nobility in her raised chin, her slender neck, the glorious sensuality of her mouth. She would not die a slave to fear, he knew, for she was a true lady of Rome.

The sound of scattering feet ravaged his thoughts. The crackle of fire. The harsh cries of brutal men.

Closer.

Ever closer.

Paulus could not keep his hand from grasping the hilt of his sword. He felt comfort in its solid contours and leather straps softened by years of sweat. Once this sword had brought him glory and position. Now it would bring him the blissful escape of death.

His eyes wandered unbidden back to Messalina. With her hair meticulously arranged, she slowly began to remove the expensive jewelry which had adorned her delicate neck and wrists since the day they were promised to each other.

Paulus could stand it no longer. He ran to her and placed his trembling hands upon the gentle slope of her neck; an enticing curve of soft, pure beauty, an elegance of line which sculptors could only dream of honoring in cold, lifeless marble. As their eyes met in the gold-framed mirror, Messalina placed a comforting hand on his. She smiled with quivering lips, her silent strength bolstering his own. There was nothing left to be said.

Nothing.

Everything had been decided weeks before. Only her simple preparations and the cruel vagaries of fate left to unfold. With a desperate moan, he buried his anguished face in her sweet-smelling hair, kissed the glistening curls with all the tumultuous love erupting from his tortured breast. For himself, he did not fear the inevitable. He was a proud soldier and statesman of the empire. Death had no power to disavow his many noble achievements. Yet, his fevered mind screamed at the thought of corruption embracing the vibrant vision that held him as he sobbed. Paulus would gladly suffer a thousand mutilations to spare his wife the indignity of the tomb. But the pleading shrieks and moans outside their once-secure home told him it was not to be.

Messalina placed an elegant hand on his cheek, and pulled him down to face her. The warm, inviting velvet of her lips fluttered healing fire and acceptance into his soul, her soft words wrapped around the turmoil of his heart, calming the maelstrom within. Her gentle voice flowed with the sweetness of warm wine over his senses.

"There are forces that even mocking Death has no dominion over, my love," she whispered with a halting tone of quiet assurance. "Our souls are joined in eternity, Paulus. And there I will find you once more." Her eyes glistened with unshed tears. "If I must search the heavens and underworld forever, I swear, my husband, I will hold you once more in my arms."

He became lost in her eyes, entranced by the serene surety of her words.

"I promise you this upon my undying love, Paulus...we will meet again."

Suddenly, he kissed her with a passion that collapsed the boundaries of time and fear. She yielded her strength through trembling lips, and the greedy caress of hopeless, unbridled love.

Afterwards, they lay together, listening with solemn detachment to the mounting chaos about to descend upon them. Messalina straightened the pale yellow silk of her dress, the errant wisps of her coal-black hair. She gazed at him for one last eternity, studying every line of his face, committing to memory every nuance of his sad, loving eyes.

"We will meet again, my love," she smiled. His stiffened resolve would allow him only to nod in reply. With painstaking delicacy, she removed the glass stopper from the small crystal vase, and placed the sparkling vial to her bruised and quivering lips.

Paulus retreated to the door, teeth clenched, as he watched the hemlock steal away all that he loved. The Roman alchemist had mixed a potent elixir of poison and narcotics, so forgiving sleep would proceed death, and thus, not ruffle her beauty as she wandered beyond the borders of life.

Messalina's eyes glazed over even before they fell upon the anguished face of her husband. She moved her mouth with words he could no longer hear, her still whispers overpowering the screams outside his door. Against his will, Paulus threw himself to her side, and as escaping life released its hold on her gentle form, he held her as she slumped backwards onto the wrinkled silk sheets.

He wanted that moment to last forever. The feel of her in his arms.

But it was not to be.

Murderous axes began to hack and splinter their door, as Paulus tenderly positioned his wife's body, as if she lay sleeping. He ignored the screams of hatred accompanying each axe blow, as he straightened the last curls of his wife's glistening black hair.

A thick, bloody arm clawed through the weakening door, as Paulus tenderly closed Messalina's lifeless eyes to the brutality soon to follow.

She door burst apart in an angry shower of wood fragments.

The barricade shifted under savage arms plump with barbarian hate.

Paulus rose, drew his hungry sword and eagerly anticipated dark vengeance and his desperate search through eternity.

****

Chilly November winds blew across the Boston College campus, scattering students like brittle autumn leaves.

Paul Marino trudged past the solemn brick buildings, burdened equally by thick textbooks and heavy emotions. He couldn't understand why he felt so...alone, so isolated in this university complex with thousands of students. Even though he had scores of friends and endless parties to attend, he continually battled that same irresistible detachment which had plagued him as far back as he could remember. He felt more an observer than a participant in his own life.

He slunk on, past pockets of happily chattering students and the occasional strolling couple, their affections proclaimed in the quiet intertwining of yearning fingers. He clenched his teeth and buried his own hands deeper into his pockets.

As he tramped toward the parking lot, he sensed his name drifting softly upon the icy breeze, which sliced through his BC jacket, mocked by the coming Massachusetts winter.

But there it was again.

'Paul...'

Distant, yet distinct.

He turned to see a girl running towards him with a soft trail of black curls flowing behind her.

"Paul," she shouted. "Paul Marino!"

For a moment, she seemed an apparition of timeless beauty. As he watched her run across the frost-tinted grounds, a curious feeling of panic and warmth overwhelmed his senses. His arm stiffened and his legs wavered. He felt a sudden need to either embrace her or run away. This was not like him. He was The Rock. The one who held the line and tortured any opponents who tried to cross the BC Eagles line of scrimmage. Yet, here he was shaking like a child for no discernible reason. And more than anything else, he did not want this strange and strangely beautiful girl to seem him so unsteady.

With a deep pull of breath, he frantically tried to shake off the disturbing sensations, and regain his composure.

"Paul," she gasped again. "Wait!"

He closed his eyes and stiffened.

It worked.

He was The Rock again.

When he opened his eyes, she was already beside him. Still, he had no idea who she was.

"Let me...catch my breath..." she wheezed. Clearly, she was not an athlete. As linebacker for the Eagles, he would have to run ten miles before he got this winded. Still, there was something oddly familiar about her.

He studied her face, cheeks reddened by cold and exertion, during the awkward silence that followed.

"Almost there," she wheezed.

"I don't mean to be rude," he said. "...but do I know you?"

She looked genuinely hurt. As she brushed the long black curls from the gentle slope of her neck, her face colored with sudden embarrassment.

"I guess not," she muttered. "I was in your Ancient History class last year...Melissa Randall."

He said nothing. Those eyes. There was something about her eyes...

"I sat in the back," she added in discomfort.

Now it was his turn to be embarrassed. "I'm sorry. I guess my mind is so stuffed with school, I uh, zone out some times. Nice to meet you."

"Like I said, we already met."

"Yeah," he kicked absently at a clump of dirt by his foot, and soon found himself staring too deeply into her dark, captivating eyes.

The hard winter ground suddenly escaped from under him, as he felt the entire campus darken and spin madly behind his eyes. He gasped at the suffocating pressure in his chest, and felt a numbness at the base of his neck slowly consume the inside of his skull. He was frightened by a loud, strangled rasping, then frightened further when he realized it was the panicked sound of his own breath.

Anguished shouts and cries of pain attacked his consciousness from unknown directions. And he knew then he was dying.

He gasped loudly, until he finally found his rescue in her face; this girl who once stood in front of him, but not really her. Those same mournful eyes, which were at once ancient and inviting. Those same mournful eyes, which suddenly seemed to rise from ivory sheets. Those same mournful eyes, smiling up at him through the haze of his whirling dementia. He lost himself in those eyes and succumbed to a creeping flush of warmth and safety.

She was speaking to him. Or was she? He couldn't be sure.

A sudden blast of bitter wind roused him, and flung him haphazardly back into the world of comfortless reality.

He gulped air, thankful only that he was still standing.

"I said, are you all right?" The strange girl...Melissa, looked up at him with frightened curiosity. He realized he was sweating. Cold, but sweating.

"Yeah," he grunted, as he carelessly wiped his forehead in a futile attempt to disguise his panic. "I, uh...I must be coming down with something."

"You look like hell."

"Thanks."

He dug his heels into the hard ground, in case the strange feeling inexplicably returned.

He refused to fall over.

Not in front of this girl.

This girl who stared up at him with transparent affection.

"Anyway," she said finally. "I've been looking for you for the longest time."

His stiffened resolve would only allow him to nod in reply. He watched her fingers - her remarkably delicate fingers -disappear inside the heavy denim backpack. They emerged with a small book bound in burnished red leather.

"My journal!" he cried, and snatched it too roughly from her hands. He leafed through it quickly, reliving all the hidden poems, intimate stories and agonizing thoughts it contained. Her voice broke his reverie.

"You left it by your desk," she muttered uncomfortably. "The last day of the semester. I've been trying to find you ever since." She let her gaze and voice descend to some elusive blade of grass.

"Did you...?" He fixed her with a stare far more brutal than he meant.

"I tried not to, but..."

"You read my journal?!" Again, his words came out much too harsh.

"Yeah...sorry..." She shifted her weight but found no added comfort. "I shouldn't have, but..." And with that, she turned and slink sadly away.

He watched her slowly make her way back to the library, saw the pale winter sun sparkle the long, dark curls which embraced her shoulders. He knew she felt him watching her, yet, he couldn't help but admire the way she held her chin up, despite her obvious embarrassment.

And then his world began to spin again. As if something deep inside him was about to die away. He turned away, unable to face her retreating back.

As he did, the giddy nausea enveloped him with a vengeance. He felt the scathing screams ravage his ears, felt his chest heave with anguish and loss. Tears rushed his eyes, as did the translucent vision of a woman's mournful face whispering words he was never to hear.

He turned back again.

"Hey!" he yelled to the girl with the heavy denim backpack. "How about a pizza?"

She stopped.

Turned slowly.

She hesitated for a brief eternity.

And when she finally did smile, Paul Marino scarcely noticed how the cold November wind had softened all around him.

WILDCAT

Daryl Lee Hargrove abruptly staggers to a rest in the center of the cavernous gymnasium, sweat matting his curly brown hair, diverting into his eyes rivulets of faux tears, and painting circles of exertion on his oversized Kentucky Wildcats T-shirt.

His narrow chest heaves and caves to the ragged music of his own breath, a raspy song of weariness and desperation. His tightened eyes rise again to the rim and net suspended above him, and he briefly imagines it looking back down upon him, taking him into account, finding him lacking. He drags a thin, sweaty forearm across his face, as he rests the large brown-orange ball against his hip, in a classic pose mimicked by nearly every high school boy across the South.

Daryl Lee is small for his fifteen years, gangly, and moves with the nervous energy of youth still uncomfortable with the sudden upward splaying of his body; often shifting in more directions at once than is necessary for simple motion.

His eyes flitter to the wispy, yellow-haired girl hunched alone in the stands, silently watching her boyfriend, her steady boyfriend, exercise out his personal demons. Even though they have been dating for only two months, she knows better than to speak when he is like this; knows her words can only savage his wounds, not soothe them.

Her eyes moisten, as he suddenly breaks and drives toward the basket to sink an easy lay-up. He trots the ball back to the three-point line and slowly bounces it on the hardwood floor, enjoying the muffled echo reverberating through the still and venerable auditorium.

"Shhh," he whispers, his words only half meant for her. "Listen."

His head tilts oddly to let the rhythmic thumping of the ball creep easily into his ear.

"Hear it? Hear that sound?"

He soaks in the reverberation, almost in awe, as the sullen heartbeat reflects off the wooden stands and matches the tortured rhythm of his chest.

He continues to dribble the ball slowly, then turns to the girl he knows will never understand, can never comprehend his passion for the game, for this place, for everything associated with the sport.

She can't possibly. After all, she's Yankee-born and bred.

"That right there is music you're hearing, Nancy. Pure, sweet music. Forget about Dixieland or the blues. This is the true music of the South. Rubber on wood. Thoom... Thoom... Thoom... Thoom... Thoom... Thoom..."

"I grew up on that sound. I grew up listenin' to folks talk about college basketball as if it was a gift from God's good heaven. I saw proud men get tears in their eyes whenever anybody speaks the name of Adolph Rupp, Joe B. Hall, Tubby Smith or John Calipari. I know fat, middle-aged men, failures all their lives, who're still treated with respect 'cause twenny or thutty years ago they was in the right place at the right time in the right game, when they got that perfect pass and sent that old ball whizzin' through the air right into the basket... Whoosh!"

He dribbles, pretends to shoot, yet, will not let the ball fly from his hand.

"Thoom... Thoom... Thoom... Whoosh!"

He looks up at her with mounting excitement, seeing stands no longer empty or silent.

"And all the crowd up and jumps to their feet. All the cryin' mothers and screamin' girlfriends, and all the daddy's so proud they could burst a collar button, all shoutin' "That's my boy! That's my boy what won the championship!"

"Whoosh! The championship game..."

"Whoosh! Immortality."

He freezes for a moment in mid-shooting pose. Slowly, he pulls back. Grips the ball between trembling fingers. His voice breaks.

"Coach told me this afternoon I didn't make the team... Said I was too short... Said I wasn't fast enough... That my heart wasn't in the game..."

He flares suddenly, staring at a coach no longer in front of him.

"What the hell does he know 'bout my heart?! What does he know 'bout how much I'd give to have all my kin up in them stands cheerin' me on at the championship game?! He don't know what that'd mean to me, seein' all my family cheerin' and hollerin' and carrying on like that! He don't know my heart. He plain don't know my heart."

Daryl Lee's head turns to the girl, staring at her in full shame.

"I'm sorry," she whispers, but he doesn't hear her. Only voices of disapproval ring in his ears.

"You know what my daddy did when I told him what the coach told me?" His voice catches. Softens to a whisper.

"My daddy spit on my hightops. He spit right on them and said I damn well better git me some heart by next season, 'cuz he damn well expects me to be on that Wildcat team someday, just like my cousin Donny was."

The boy swats away the liquid emotion that betray his eyes.

"I ain't never seen daddy so mad."

They each shrunk into the silence. The small boy on the large wooden court and the heartbroken girl alone in the stands. Their eyes meet, mist with emotion, and he briefly wonders if maybe she can understand a little. How desperately he needs someone to understand. His voice sinks to a level she can barely hear, but the lack of words doesn't lessen the communication between them.

"I am gonna make it next year, Nancy... I'm gonna be a Wildcat one day. I give you my word on that.

She does not doubt him.

"'Cuz basketball, see, it's my whole life."

She nods, and he knows she understands.

Daryl Lee Hargrove bounces the orb of dreams by his worn sneakers, listening carefully to its dull, echoing beat.

"Hear that, Nancy?"

"Thoom... Thoom... Thoom..."

"That's the sound of my heart there. Take a listen."

And she does.

She always will.

KNOWING WHEN TO LEAVE

The trick, he decided, was knowing when to leave.

A good entrance might impress, but it can quickly be upstaged by the next good entrance. What you say in normal conversation is usually forgotten, what you do is seldom enough for most people.

But knowing when to leave, yes, knowing when to cut and run, that was the trick. A strong exit will always leave a lasting impression. Leave them wanting more, instead of the incremental horror of growing indifference. On this simple strategy, Anthony Manley had built his life.

Perhaps life was too strong a word for his well-choreographed series of abbreviated relationships and well-timed exits. As Anthony stared, red-eyed and vulnerable, into the coldly mocking gaze of his bathroom mirror, he knew he had over-stayed yet another welcome. He could see it in the somber gray wash of his jowls, the humorless crinkle of his once-dancing eyes, the downward slump of his too-easy smile. The fifty year-old face that stared back at him was daunting in its accusation.

He had broken the ground rules.

He had stayed too long.

His eyes caught a flicker of blue flannel in the reflection behind him, and he jumped at the sudden intrusion of her words.

"What the hell are you doing, staring into the mirror like that?" The was pure Shannon, a question forged in annoyance, lacking in curiosity.

He watched her watching him, and had no answer to give. Their eyes met in the icy otherworld of the mirror's reflection, as if each was a stranger to be observed with mild interest, no physical connection.

"So?"

"So…what?" he cringed, unsure of what failures today had in store.

"Are you going to get Julie up, or not?" Shannon asked, while lowering herself onto the toilet.

He nodded, slapped a handful of painfully cold water against his burning cheeks and grunted in reply. Morning discourse in the Manley home. They both knew that conversations in a dying marriage, like water, always sought the path of least resistance.

As she watched her husband trudge expressionless from his perch by the bathroom mirror, Shannon Manley felt the familiar twinge of emptiness which had become her too-frequent companion over the last ten years. She wiped, flushed, then stared into her own mirror, a half bathroom away from his, and wondered again how she would make it through another day, trapped within the desiccating embrace of this uninhabited marriage. She had long ago tired of trying, his inner chaos too much to share.

****

Anthony moved quietly into the darkened room, and stared at the sleeping nine-year-old who sprawled so largely now in the tangled chaos of Little Mermaid sheets and pillows. Stuffed animals crawled across the bed, all watching him watching her. His precious child Melissa had grown in desperate fits and starts, always it seemed, while he was looking elsewhere, so that he was constantly surprised by how quickly she slipped towards adulthood, all the while slipping away from him.

If only he had taken more time to be a father, instead of using his time being a listening ear to some other pathetically emotional cripple. He watched her breathe, a soft gentle puff of warm air through pouty child lips, a slight dash and flutter of eyes behind closed lashes, seeing dreams too quickly forgotten in the stark glare of pre-teen pressures and adolescent acceptability. She frowned, perhaps sensing his presence, turned awkwardly on her side, and dug her tiny face deeper into the pillow than he would have thought possible.

"Time to get up, sweetheart." he whispered, dropping a kiss on her sweat tousled hair. "Please wake up, Melissa."

No response at all. He placed a hand on her thin shoulder.

"Sweetheart... Please wake up for Daddy..."

It was useless, he knew. Perhaps she was feigning sleep. Perhaps she had subconsciously dismissed him years ago, made him all but invisible. Somewhere along the line between Daddy's little girl and Mommy's staunch ally, she had grown hardened by overhearing too many marital meltdowns, and vowed she would never let a man, any man, ever get close enough to wound her. From that point on, Anthony had lost the ability to wake his daughter for school. He would begin with soft whispers and tender kisses, then escalate to gentle shaking, vigorous jostling, and finally, yells and threats of spanking. For her mother, it was different. Shannon would softly climb into bed with Melissa, wrap her flannel-softened arms around the sleeping child, and his daughter would rise with the first whispered, "Wake up, my precious baby."

Shannon got the morning smiles. Anthony earned the morning scowls and defiance.

He could not bear it this morning. Especially not this morning. He jostled her once more, received no discernible response, then turned from the room in silent surrender. Shannon would berate him for abrogating his parental duties, he knew, but he had no heart for Melissa's tears today. Not today of all days. Better to have the child love her mother, than to acquire yet another excuse to hate the poor excuse for a father he had become.

How strange, he thought, picking at unseen lint on his shirt.

He once believed he had all the potential to be the most wonderful father on earth, had for a while fooled himself into thinking he had achieved that distinction, and at times even allowed brief glimpses of that vulnerable, nurturing person within to escape, overcoming his whirlpool of fears and emotional barricades. Yet, mocking Nature always moves toward a balance, and the void in his soul was gradually reflected in the increasing hollowness of his family relationships. He was a stick figure in a three-dimensional world, easily ignored, easily crumbled; a father of consequence on government forms only. He closed his daughter's bedroom door and pretended to busy himself in the kitchen. A deserter once more.

A clock ticked loudly, stealing away seconds that had no meaning, no direction, no value.

It was 8:23 AM when Melissa scurried off to the bus stop, and Anthony's thoughts turned once again to escape. When you have nothing left to offer, he reasoned, a sudden disappearance was the best defense in the world. As he mixed the special ingredients in his morning coffee, Anthony Manley knew it was time to leave.

He knew he had to leave because the people he was closest to had finally become as unreal to him as he had to them, shadows moving without substance through the dark and light of his life, like images projected on the walls of his kitchen, his ironically named family room, his office, his bedroom; all painfully fascinating to watch, yet impossible to hold, unlikely to offer even the slightest shred of comfort or warmth.

He sipped his bitter coffee and realized everybody in his life was like that to him now. He watched them from within an insulating window of self-pity; observed them go through the trajectory of their lives, never noting his emotional absence.

Perhaps they chose not to notice. Perhaps it was just too painful. Perhaps, they loved the facade of intimacy too much. It was simpler that way, easier to digest; for with Anthony Manley, all intimacy had become a chest-tightening illusion.

Only at a few points in his life, would a select few attempt to pierce his steel-nettled veil. They would ask to see the real him, insist on it, upbraid him when he held back, then be gradually repulsed when he revealed, in unpalatable morsels, who he really was inside. So it had always been for Anthony. Names and faces would change, reactions never did. After a glowing burst of attraction sparked by enigmatic eyes, smiles would fade, and love would follow. Soon they would distance themselves from this inner him with a sad "You've changed, Anthony."

But he hadn't changed.

He had merely revealed.

Perhaps if he had offered his wife as much as he had offered his recent succession of empty friendships, his marriage might have survived this dizzying spiral into animosity. If he had only been there for her half as much as he had for the 'tangentals,' as he called them, the spiritually damaged who gravitated to him as eagerly as he sought them out; a fellowship of the fragile that soon came to define all his relationships. He exchanged friendships for voices of discontent. Interaction for observation. There was nothing mutual in the connections he fostered; he might as well have been a dial-in therapist, for he listened without empathy, soothed without concern, and felt no need to reveal any portion of his own identity, which was acceptable since they were not there for him and did not require him to be there for them, not really. They were mushrooms nurtured from the decaying heart of a fallen tree. As long as he smiled and nodded and exhibited all the facial manifestations of understanding, these tangentals were content to unleash their litany of troubles upon him. Then, temporarily cleansed, they would return to other relationships of greater substance.

For his part, Anthony was content with the delusion that he was interacting with others of his species. He felt it much easier to listen to those whose suffering wasn't so close to his heart, whose pain he had not caused.

All these thoughts swirled before his consciousness like dry leaves in the wind, and he felt even less tied to the ground.

Anthony coughed violently over the steaming liquid that coursed down his throat, then gradually forced himself to stillness once again. His thoughts returned to Shannon. He would miss losing her more than any of the others. She alone had instilled in him the tortured ember of hope and redemption. Something he never learned to instill in himself.

She alone.

He knew it was really over between them when Shannon suddenly disappeared from his dreams. Not just those vague or specific longings for the future, her presence had vanished from all his night-time encounters, as if the constant misfire of his daily emotions barred her from entering his subconscious flights of imagination and desire. Once she had played a central role in all his dreams, nightmares, or erotic musings. Her ethereal image was his constant companion, ever at his side to stare down any horrific challenge the night would present, or to add sensual warmth to any tender moment. He could remember the erotic dreams in exquisite detail, vivid in their palette of sensations. Even in his dreams, he could smell her fragrance, feel the warming velvet of her skin, and drink in the image of her face with wakeful alertness.

Over time, she had dissolved from his dreams, replaced by a large cast of others. They were not shadows, but real women, at least he hoped they were, though he had never met any of them. Yet, they were not just faces and bodies. They were emotionally complex women who helped him face the challenges she once did. Defeating creatures or evil pursuers with a blend of courage, fear and faithfulness that matched his own, amorous lovers whose bodies were fresh and inviting, yet were secondary to the rarefied feelings of love they triggered in him. It was more erotic to have these women simply want him to hold them than to make love to them, although, in truth, he often did make love to them with a passion he now only found in dreams. Yet, he would be grateful to have them merely settle in his arms. Their faces, young or old, always changing, always looking up at him with the same shading of kindness and trembling trust. An outpouring of love that would remain with him long after he woke and confronted his day. He would remember the soft curve of a face, feel the pain of a tragically unreal paramour, and search vainly in the conscious world for her counterpart.

But she was never there.

In cold reality, he found only his wife, and she in turn, was never there in his dreams, just as he was no longer there for her in reality. *How cruel the world could be,* he thought. How mocking in its frivolous irony. He sipped another mouthful of the bitter coffee and winced, his thoughts retreating and regathering in alternate waves of sorrow and self-contempt.

Shannon had been married when he first met her, although not technically. She and her first husband shared a palatial estate in upper New York. He lived on the top floor, she on the bottom. She had long ago filed a writ of separation. They maintained separate cars, separate careers, separate bedrooms, separate dreams. It was a marriage in all but the actual sense. Neither willing to take that step off the cliff of formal divorce. Instead, they moved through each other's lives like ghosts, haunted each other's existence with bitter memories and unexpressed bile.

When he met Shannon, Anthony did not even know she was married. When he did find out she was legally separated, he did not care. He did not care that she still shared the house with her husband. It was adultery in all but the legal sense.

In retrospect, Anthony's punishment had been tragically poetic. Shannon had been drawn to him for his fun-loving, dangerous nature. He had been attracted to her for her smoldering sensuality and constantly optimistic way of looking at the world. If only she could escape this atrophied first marriage, if only she could begin life again, what promise the future would hold for them both! Anthony and Shannon made love like incendiary devices, as if their entire lives might be gloriously consumed in the act. Now, years later, mortgage, marriage and child had squeezed the dangerous side from him, leaving him far closer to the specter of her first husband, a fact she was eager to point out at all of his most vulnerable moments. The optimism and positive strength he so admired had, bit by bit, been replaced by the language of continuous complaint. A non-stop stream of dissatisfaction, more poignant because she did not even realize she was saying it. They conversed in the softly violent dialect of shattered dreams, each word underscored by accusatory disappointment.

As for their incendiary love-making, it had indeed consumed all spark between them. All that was left was a once-a-month ritual that bore no similarity to the woman he wrested from her previous life. He once overheard her grumble to a friend on the telephone that "she could easily do without it for the rest of her life." Now those words – delivered to another, but meant for him to hear - stalked him on the monthly occasions she did open herself to him in the dark.

I am an obligation, he thought. Not a lover, but a chore.

She made love to him, as she had her first husband, skillfully but mechanically. If only he had realized sex for her was not a physical act, but a pouring out of all the tenderness and love she felt for him. That was where she got her pleasure. It had become too painful for her to feel anything for him, holding him in her arms imagining that he would rather be holding someone else. Telling her to "grow up" when she tried to discuss her pain or concerns, all the while listening to others with compassion enough to fill entire rooms.

What she needed most was a friend, like the kind of friend he could only be to the tangentals, those who told him he was wonderful for caring; like she would, if only he did.

As he drained the last of his sour coffee, he closed his eyes and briefly caught a glimpse of their wedding. The smiles, the hopes, the tenderness of that day so long ago. But it was too elusive to last, too fragile to endure. And that thought enhanced the constriction in his throat.

The same people who often talked until dawn with the voracious curiosity of new love, now communicated for weeks at a time solely in nods, glares and softly muttered obscenities. What they had lost was crippling to consider, so they each avoided doing so at every opportunity. There was a gaping wound across their marriage, infecting the basic goodness they originally discovered in each other's soul. But they refused to speak of it. For recognizing the affliction would force them into a healing that was far more frightful than the disease.

And what he was doing now was the only way out.
He did not want to leave a note.
He couldn't.
He had nothing left to say.

As he hoped, the arsenic did not take long to reach his heart. He felt, but did not feel, his forehead slam into the table. In a panic, he desperately hoped his daughter would not find his body first and try in vain to wake him. That would be too cruel.
He hoped it would be Shannon.

Shannon who would understand what he had done.

Shannon, who would simply know it was Anthony's time to leave.

THE GOOD SAMARITAN

The engagement arrived exactly as planned, the lavish wedding went off without a hitch, but after five and a half months, Lorraine Hudson Duvall realized the marriage had lasted far too long.

As she brushed her long, glistening hair in front of the gold-trimmed mirror, Lorraine tried to calculate where precisely she had gone wrong. The ornate brush glided through her ash-blonde hair like a gilded surfer coasting on a sun-tinted ocean wave. The soft incandescent bulbs which framed the oversized mirror had been specially placed to cast a mischievous twinkle in her jade green eyes. Those eyes were troubled now, the aesthetic manifestation of plans gone awry.

Lorraine lowered the gold brush onto her crystal vanity, and began applying moisturizing cream to the small worry lines beginning to form around her wide, expressive eyes.

"Damn him!" she muttered out loud. "This is all his fault!"

And indeed, it was. Twenty-seven was far too young for worry lines, especially on a woman in as exquisite shape as she was. If he had only died on time, she would have been free to enjoy the uncomplicated lifestyle she was sure she so richly deserved. Instead, she had to smile sweetly through his nightly leering, his ice-cold touch, and the interminable stories of his own inexorable rise to power. Ancient history, as far as Lorraine was concerned. Forbes and Fortune had written his life story time and again. He was a legend. An icon. A financial pirate.

A true American success story.

She had to bite her lip to keep from gagging each and every time he chose to relive those endless tales of corporate cunning, which had transformed the blue collar boy from New Jersey into one of the twenty richest men in America.

The cruel shudder which passed between her shoulders was a direct response to the new image that abruptly appeared in the gilded mirror.

R. Jefferson Duvall's cadaverous face suddenly loomed, a ghostly reflection which hovered over the startled features of his lovely wife. Lorraine spun around and faced the man at the bedroom door.

"Darling," he drawled in his fashionable, pseudo-Southern tones. "Henri has informed me that dinner has been laid out on the table for some time now. In fact, he says it's getting cold."

Oooh, how she hated him! The sunken eyes, the faint aroma of decay, the pale flesh of his cheeks, which sagged gray and ghastly pink to his jawline, the tired eyes that moaned of impending death. A death delayed much too long, as far as Lorraine was concerned. It took all her strength to force a smile in his direction, but when it finally did sweep across her face, he interpreted it as an expression both alluring and full of love.

"Thank you, sweetness. I'll be with you in half a moment." Again, the smile glowed, a weapon she had always wielded with deadly precision.

He was appropriately smitten.

"Wonderful, darling. I'll be waiting." As he backed out of the doorway, he looked almost pitiful, this wretched old man so infatuated with the smile of a girl less than a third his age. Lorraine felt a momentary twinge of compassion for the aged fool, who deluded himself into believing a woman like her could actually fall in love with a shuffling anachronism like him. Yet, the twinge of sympathy was quickly replaced by a wave of bitterness, as she again relived the touch of his frigid hands.

"Why me?" she sighed softly to the mirror, but it offered her no compassion.

****

The twenty-six foot Edwardian table dominated the opulent dining room, a massive hall lavishly festooned with hand-carved cherubim and floor-to-ceiling English tapestries. The ornate crystal and gold chandelier was imported a decade earlier from the once-elegant castle of a bankrupt Bavarian nobleman. The Eighteenth Century china was the last of its kind, aggressively sought after by seven international museums. The wine was Saint-Emillion Premier Grand Cru classé, a prized 1967 vintage from Chateau Monbousquet. The dinner was Osso Bucco, served in generous portions.

The conversation was virtually non-existent.

Although they failed to notice, the two people in the room were dwarfed by the grandeur which enveloped them. They sat on opposite ends of the long table, too far apart for Duvall to hear his young wife's muttered diatribe.

"What was that you said, my darling?" She could have been talking much louder and the results would have been the same. R. Jefferson Duvall steadfastly refused to wear the hearing aid his doctor had supplied. *Makes me look vulnerable...'* he thought.

"I said, have you had any more of those awful chest pains, dearest?" Under the golden glow of the antique chandelier, her perfect face swam like a vision of loveliness within the old man's moist eyes. The tender concern of his beautiful, young wife was like a balm to his soul...a soul that had witnessed too much ugliness in its time, and perpetrated even more.

But she was more than beautiful. Jefferson Duvall saw her as the rebirth of his own manhood, a rare and wondrous treasure too precious to display, except of course, to those chosen business associates he would allow to envy him. They would see his resurgent vitality in her unflagging devotion. What power she afforded him, in ways her untrained mind could not possibly fathom.

Yet, as much as she was a quantifiable asset in his prestige portfolio, his heart knew her as something more. Something indefinable. A person of warmth and character in a world grown sadly sterile from the endless bombardment of corporate politics and controlling interests. She was real in his eyes. Genuine in spirit, where he had fabricated defenses. Soft in exactly the places he was hard. Duvall was in love, and he knew it. He knew he could one day become hopelessly lost in her eyes, and remain content to stare at her perfectly sculpted face forever.

Now, he merely grimaced as he looked down at the remainder of his meal. He hated playing the love-struck fool. He hated any sign of weakness.

"Not too many. Nothing to worry about," His words hard and abrupt. "I can wring another twenty years out of this old body. No damn doctor's gonna tell me otherwise!"

The young woman watched her aged husband bow his head to slowly chew his veal. She knew the pain he felt in his jaw, the poor digestion, the nightly constrictions in his chest. She knew, because she had seen his medical records months before she had seen his face.

Lorraine Hudson had spent four enlightening months as an administrative assistant in the medical offices of Dr. Timothy O'Rourke, one of Bel Aire's leading heart specialists. The beautiful young girl from Indiana had seduced O'Rourke as easily as all the others. The progression was always the same; an innocent glance, an inadvertent touch, a shy smile, a breathless hesitation, and finally, an uninhibited rush of sublime passion. After just one well-orchestrated interlude, she had gained unfettered access to all his patient's files. She had allotted four months to find the perfect husband...vain, elderly, excessively wealthy, widowed, and suffering from a terminal heart condition.

In less than three weeks, she had found the file of R. Jefferson Duvall, determined he was exactly what she would need, and began plotting her seduction of the world-famous financier.

One night, she found herself alone with him in the elevator, not cold, but too proud to be easily charmed by his simple flattery. She left him only a soft 'thank you' in response to his gushing appreciation of her beauty. Then, as she stepped off the elevator, she turned back to him with a smile that fluttered his heart as no woman had done in thirty or more years. After which, she vanished amid the shadows of the underground parking lot.

She made sure she was working the front desk for his regular check-up one month later. She regarded him with less distance now, as if the secret smile on the elevator had somehow bridged a great gulf between them. A flirtatious conspiracy was born. In subsequent meetings, she became more and more accessible. In this way, he became convinced he was gradually winning her over with his inimitable charm.

There was no room in her plans for urgency. When he finally asked her out for dinner, she gently refused, though she would not tell him why. The next time he asked, she hesitated, then refused, but tenderly explained that she still suffered from a deep romantic wound. She would reveal no further details. When he at last invited her out for a quick cup of coffee, she accepted his offer with glee. In the crowded cafeteria, she wove a story of a wild, young lover who had taken her innocence, then dashed her heart on the jagged rocks of callous indifference. She could not bear the pain of indifference in a lover's eye ever again. When he said he understood, she could not help but brush his wrinkled hand with her delicate fingers.

Electricity.

Two months later, despite ever-softening protestations, she allowed herself to be seduced in the back of his stretch limousine. Her first moan of passion was a cry of victory. They were married one month later in a quiet ceremony attended only by four hundred carefully selected subordinates and business associates.

R. Jefferson Duvall never knew he had won the heart of this exceptional woman in a game that was rigged from the start.

Now, she stared down twenty-six feet of Edwardian splendor to the ninety-three year-old man who firmly believed he possessed her, body and soul. She noticed his pale hand shake as he raised a fork to his cold, cracked lips. She observed how his dull gray hair absorbed more light than it reflected. And she desperately looked for signs of the heart condition which was supposed to spare her from his continuing attention. At that moment, he noticed her eyes upon him, and he smiled in return.

"You are so breathtakingly beautiful, Lorraine," He whispered, no longer able to prevent the deluge of emotion from seeping into his voice. "Only with you here beside me do I feel like a rich man."

Lorraine's eyes sparkled with wine and insight. Suddenly, she knew what she had to do to take care of her ailing husband.

"Sweetness..." she beamed back at him. "I've decided to take a course in CPR."

****

Lorraine leaned over the rubber mannequin with the exposed chest cavity. Ambulatory Annie was actually only half a body, specially designed for CPR training. Lorraine grasped the back of her left hand with her right, interlocked her knuckles, and applied straight-armed pressure to the mannequin's chest. She leaned into the rhythm, at a rate of thirty thrusts per minute.

"Hold on there, little lady. You're trying to help Annie here, not wrestle her."

The criticism was made infinitely more palatable by the ruggedly handsome face smiling up at her. Justin was a local fireman, who volunteered to teach CPR, cardiopulmonary resuscitation, once a month.

He usually sleepwalked through the eight-hour workshop, but when he saw Lorraine Hudson Duvall, he actually envied the dummies. She was the most beautiful woman he had ever seen, outside of a magazine centerfold, and here he was, teaching her how to give a rubber mannequin the kiss of life. Her shy smile made it difficult for him to concentrate on any of his other students. The low-cut blouse and tight pants she wore made this monthly volunteer effort all worthwhile.

Still leaning over the mannequin, Lorraine looked up at him with a surprised expression.

"What did I do wrong, Mister Houglan?"

He loved the way she said his name, could picture her saying it every morning of his life. Could picture her...ah, but the class was beginning to notice his...distraction.

"Well, Lorraine," he tried to sound official, though he felt like giggling. "For one thing, you forgot to check for a pulse before you initiated CPR. If Annie here had a pulse to start with, you could actually stop her heart by compressing her chest with a contrary rhythm. Your hands are in the wrong place and you're pushing much too hard. You can crack a rib, or do severe damage to the chest cavity like that. Also, your rhythm's way too fast."

Her face fell with the cutest look of dejection he had ever seen. She looked up at him with childlike innocence.

"Other than all that...how did I do?" Her soft humor was the perfect touch. If only he wasn't happily married. If only he didn't have four kids he worshipped. If only...

"Well, just keep on practicing, Lorraine," he smiled. "I know you'll get the hang of it." Houglan also knew it was time he turned away from the clumsy goddess and devoted at least a portion of the remaining time to his other students. How could she get a perfect score on the written part of the CPR test, yet do everything so wrong in practice? How could such an incredibly sexy woman be so...

He shook his head at his own foolishness. In an hour, she'd be gone, and he would return to a life filled with love and personal contentment.

Yet, a part of him would remember that warm smile and those stunning green eyes for years to come.

****

In the darkness of their master bedroom, Lorraine listened intently to the soft snoring which floated upwards from the far side of the king-sized bed. A heavy snorer, Jefferson Duvall was breathing unevenly tonight. Perhaps it was exhaustion from the heavy birthday routine she had scheduled for him. Fifty select friends wishing him a happy ninety-fourth. A bit too much wine to wash down an unusually heavy dinner. A bottle of champagne shared alone in the bedroom, long after the drunken guests had departed. Then, an hour of vigorous love-making that left the aging tycoon gulping for air.

It was Duvall's best birthday in years, but a cardiologist's worst nightmare.

Henri the cook and Edgar the valet both insisted on staying the night. Perhaps they could sense the danger in the extended celebration. Perhaps they had noticed their employer's abnormally gray color, as his young wife led him up to bed. Yet, Mrs. Duvall insisted they leave. On a special night like this, she wanted to be alone with her husband. She assured them she could take care of her husband.

Now, in the dark, Lorraine heard the sudden catch of his breath, the soft gasping rattle in his throat. There was no time to lose. She rolled her sleeping husband onto his back, placed her palms on the center of his rib cage, and began to administer CPR as fast as she possibly could.

****

In the interrogation room of the Bel Aire police station, Detective Javier Branniff stared down a cigarette at the most beautiful woman he had seen this week. It had been three days since the funeral of R. Jefferson Duvall, and the new widow looked remarkably composed.

Too composed.

She had not raised any objections, or even surprise, when he had asked her to come down to the station for a few questions. This one was cool as a cucumber, and twice as tasty.

"Mrs. Duvall," he began again. "I know this is a real tough time for you, but I have to get some of this clear in my head. When precisely did you start cardiopulmonary resuscitation on your late husband?"

"It was 3:15 in the morning. Approximately. I was a little too distracted to look at the clock."

"And again, what made you decide to initiate CPR?"

"As I told you, he stopped breathing. He had a long history of heart problems, and I didn't want to take any chances."

"Did you check for a pulse first?"

"I don't know. I assume so, but it all happened so quickly, I don't remember."

Detective Branniff stood up and slowly paced around the steel table with the peeling wood veneer. This would have to be handled very carefully. The widow Duvall was now a very powerful woman, politically. He packaged his question with every ounce of sympathy he could muster.

"Mrs. Duvall...you know what kind of injuries your husband sustained from your efforts to revive him, don't you?"

"I heard he had a bruised heart, plus a number of cracked ribs, one of which pierced his right lung." She said it simply, as calmly as if she was discussing the weather with a stranger. "I might have been a bit overzealous in my efforts to revive him."

Branniff coughed out a laugh.

"Overzealous? An eight-hundred pound gorilla couldn't have been more overzealous! The truth is, the coroner determined it was injuries from your CPR, not any type of heart attack, that actually killed your husband. Would you consider that a little overzealous?"

"I must have panicked in the excitement of the situation."

"Excitement? Did you say 'the excitement' of the situation?"

"Poor choice of words. I meant the anxiety of the situation."

"Of course, you did."

She stood up and walked over to him. That knowing look. The chilling smile. The studied way in which she casually touched his arm with her hand. This was a cool one, all right.

"I'm CPR certified, Detective," She smiled seductively, just inches from his face. "I guess I'm just not very good at it."

"Oh. I think you are, Mrs. Duvall," He had to step away from her, regain his breath and his composure. "I think you're exceedingly good at everything you do. I pulled your marks on the CPR exam you took two weeks ago. You answered every question right on the written exam. Every one. One hundred percent. Yet, when it came to using that knowledge to save the life of your ninety-four year-old husband, you suddenly became a cross between an Olympic weightlifter and the Three Stooges. Why do you think that is, Mrs. Duvall?"

She did not register the slightest change in her expression.

Not a twinge. Not an eye movement. Perfectly in control.

"You'll have to ask my lawyer, Detective." That smile again. "If you feel you have a case, that is."

Lorraine Hudson Duvall picked up her purse and sauntered across the interrogation room to the door. She was about to grab the knob, when she suddenly turned back to him.

"You think I murdered my husband, don't you, Detective Branniff?"

He hesitated for only a moment.

"Off the record?"

"Off the record."

The gloves were off, he thought. Let's see if she can take a punch. He began with fire.

"Off the record, I think you executed your feeble old husband to get your hands on his twenty-two billion without him having to get his feeble old hands on you. I think the one thing you learned most of all in that CPR class was the Good Samaritan law we have in this state."

"The Good Samaritan law?"

"That little statute that says anyone certified to perform CPR cannot be sued or prosecuted for attempting to resuscitate a victim in distress. It's a good law that protects real heroes. But I think you found out about it, and turned it into something dirty. I think you didn't try to revive a victim. I think you made a victim out of a sleeping man. I think you wore the old guy out with that party and lots of liquor, then you waited until he was sleeping so soundly that you could get in a few good crunches to the chest to stop his heart. I wouldn't be surprised if he even woke up while you were in the act of killing him."

"Gosh, you must think I'm pretty terrifying to do all that to my own husband."

A cool one. No doubt about it. Branniff had to be impressed. "Terrifying? You scare me to death, lady," he muttered.

"Good," she smiled again, a Cheshire Cat grin. "I think I like that."

Detective Javier Branniff could not let her get away like that. He reached for her arm. She did not pull away from his rough grasp.

"Did you do it, Lorraine? Did you kill your husband?"

She hesitated...looked deep into his intent brown eyes. Slowly, her mood seemed to change, to soften.

"Off the record?" she whispered.

"Sure."

She leaned in close to him. So close her breasts brushed his arm, and her hair fell lightly on his neck. Her lips hovered less than an inch from his ear. So close, he could feel her warm, sensual breath coursing through his veins. She spoke in a voice so soft, it trapped his own breath deep within him.

"Ask my lawyer..." she whispered.

Then, she smiled sweetly and walked out of the interrogation room.

****

That night, Lorraine Hudson Duvall, one of the twenty richest people in America, sat before her vanity brushing her long, blonde hair. She leaned closer to examine something new in her reflection.

Then she smiled.

There were no longer any worry lines around her jade green eyes.

UNBUCKLING THE BIBLE BELT

"Sweet Jesus, I have seen the face of temptation and its name is Bourbon Street!

Now, you know, Lord, I've always been a God-fearing, Bible-studyin' Christian...but why did you have to lead me down to that particular den of inequity? I mean, who's all-fired bright idea was it to schedule a church deacon's convention in the heart of New Orleans?!

There we was, prayin' and plannin' and doin' Your good work in Your good name for eight solid hours... We was all fired up about the new choir hymnals and the resolution to extend the right hand of Christian brotherhood to those heathen Catholics, by attendin' their Friday Fish Fry twice a year. We was doin' inspired work, Lord. Inspired work...right up until that Lucifer-in-disguise, Brother Ornell from Murfreesboro, suggested we adjourn early and go preach some redemption to those sinners up in the French Quarter.

Well...It seemed like a good idea at the time...

So, off we go...me, Brother Ornell, Brother Dixon and ten or twelve more of your faithful servants, marching down to Bourbon Street with fire in our eyes, the Good Book in our hands, and songs of praise on our lips. We was born again that night, let me tell you!

We marched like the personification of Your wrath straight into Sodom and Gomorrah. Brother Ornell, he starts preachin' the Word to this wino rollin' around by the curb. Brother Dixon spies a gaggle of Japanese tourists, and takes off after them with a vengeance. All the other deacons find a sinner or two of their own to bring back to Your bosom, and they take off in all different directions...there ain't bein' no shortage of sinners down there in the French Quarter.

Me... I spy the back of a little black-haired child in one of those red-laced woman things that clung to her form like sweet mornin' dew on a watermelon. She's standin' there in her shameful outfit, like Jezebel from the Old Testament, tryin' to lure the wicked and the weak with her feminine wiles. Only no one's responding, 'cuz there's a Jezebel just like her in every doorway.

So I walk up behind her and say to her in my deepest, God-fearing tones, I say "Repent, sinner! Forsake thy evil ways!" And I start quotin' Book and Verse to her in my most powerful, Sunday meeting hall voice, so as to scare away any poor souls who might be lured to her doorway.

Suddenly, she turns to me with a face as pure and pretty as an angel...and somehow all those Scriptures I quoted a thousand times get all caught up in my throat like month-old jambalaya!

There I stood, wavin' my Bible on Bourbon Street, struck dumb by the most beautiful face anyone ever turned in my direction...mounted on a body only the devil coulda fashioned with its amazin' power over the male of the species!

I'm trying to look straight into her wide, blue eyes in order to convince her of my determination to save her very soul...but my own married eyes start strayin' to places they ain't even supposed to be visitin'!

Then, by some unholy power, as I'm lookin' at this lovely incarnation of sinfulness...every Scripture passage I know as well as my own name flies straight outa my head and high-tails it to parts unknown! She's smilin' up at me with those soft painted lips...and suddenly the only sacred words I can remember from your Good Book is the Seventh Commandment... "Thou shalt not commit adultery."

So there I am, made dumb-struck and foolish by this lovely dark-haired child in her red-laced devil's finery, shoutin' over and over again: "Thou shalt not commit adultery! Thou shalt not commit adultery! Thou shalt not commit adultery! Thou shalt not commit adultery!"

And she looks up at me with a smile that melts my backbone, and whispers... "But I ain't married, sugar."

"Sugar," she calls me...Sugar was the word, and sugar was the way it slipped past her soft, cherry-red lips. All of a sudden, my heart begins poundin' away like a Salvation Army drum band, and I have to stagger back against the concrete doorway, or I'm sure to fall flat on my faith...uh, I mean face...fall flat on my face.

Then this Jezebel, who's real name is Tiffany I find out later, starts telling me how she always admired the passion us men of the cloth have whenever we were talk about the Good Book. She says the word 'passion' like it was the very phrase that made Eve chomp right down on that apple, way back when in the Garden of Eden. Here I am, half-collapsed in the doorway and I'm staring back at that angelic face, and start thinkin' about old Eve wearing nothing but a fig leaf, and I just break out in a cold sweat. I surely do. I tell you, I felt every bit like a slow-runnin' turkey on Thanksgiving!

I turn my head to look away from those hypnotic eyes, and I see, all around me, your flock in disarray. Brother Ornell was havin' such a good productive talk with his designated sinner, he's carried it on inside a nightclub and is buying the next round. Brother Dixon is wearin' Mickey Mouse ears and posin' for pictures with all those Japanese tourists, while Brothers Wyatt and Isaiah are dancin' and singin' karaoke songs in the middle of Bourbon Street!

Maybe we was tired from our trip and all, but, dear Lord, I ain't never, in all my born days, seen so many fall so far, so fast! The score looked like Sinners - Twelve, and the Righteous about to be shut out for sure!

Now Tiffany smiles real pretty-like, and turns those soft, warm eyes back on me, with a look that could melt concrete. I don't even try to talk anymore, because every time I look into that face, I'm trippin' over my tongue worse than a frog in high heels.

Then, this beautiful child, this vision of pure loveliness...starts to lean over, like she's gonna kiss me right there in the doorway!

What else could I do, Lord? I ran as fast as I could back to my hotel room and called my wife back in Paducah, and told her I was comin' home on the very next plane outta New Orleans!

Hoooeeey! They don't call that town 'The Big Easy' for nothin'!

Lord, I have seen the very face of temptation. I have felt the sweet kiss of its hot breath on my soul.

I never told anyone but you about my turmoil... But it did seem a might strange that Brother Ornell, Brother Dixon and a passle of the other deacons also cut their stay short and grabbed that very next plane flight outta New Orleans.

We was a quiet bunch on that plane, let me tell you, each man lost in his own reflections. The only thing we did talk about was how next year's convention was going to be held somewhere more...appropriate.

And as far away from The Big Easy as humanly possible!"

DAGGER REBORN

This wasn't him. This wasn't like him at all.

It was as if someone, or something, had taken over his body and brought him to this strange place to do all these bizarre things.

He shifted uncomfortably in his upholstered seat, and gripped the steering wheel with his massive, scarred hands.

It wasn't him, he kept on telling himself, and somehow that made it all easier to bear. He knew who he was and wasn't afraid to admit it. Dagger Lawrence, bad-ass personified. If you needed someone broken into little pieces, Dagger was your man.

But this...no, this just wasn't him.

He was never one of those people who had to go out and 'find themselves,' only to be saddened or embarrassed by the shallowness or cruelty they eventually uncovered inside. Dagger never had any problem knowing who he was. He had been accused of many things in his arrogant romp through this undersized world, but being deep, mysterious or complex was not among them. His bold swagger was not an affectation, but a method of announcing his presence which had propelled him forward from the first moment he wore shoes. To tell the truth, he got a kick out of the way strangers' eyes would widen with fear whenever he stomped into a room, or whenever he needed to get into someone's face.

Dagger Lawrence had shoulders as wide as Texas; a long, black and gray ponytail that snaked down between his shoulder blades; and a look of pure, unbridled fury which could make a rabid gorilla weep. He was two hundred forty-nine pounds, six foot, three-and-a-half inches of ice cold vengeance on a stick. He lived for the days people would snicker "You're not as tough as you look," but no one who valued the ability to speak dared express that sentiment anymore.

He had earned the name Dagger after some biker punk tried to cut him up for stealing his girlfriend. The knife flashed dangerously close to Dagger's face, which only got him madder. He reached out, open-handed, and grabbed the blade by sticking it straight though his own palm, which enabled him to jerked it right out of the grip of the surprised assailant. Then, with his one unbloodied hand, he beat the biker so unmercifully, the man had never been able to eat solid food again.

That was the real Dagger Lawrence.

Not this alien thing behind the wheel, driving back from hell and into a future twice as bleak.

Dagger was hard and fast and damned proud of it. When he was young, he was fast enough to dodge the heavy wooden cane his father would often use as an "learning tool and attitude adjuster." And he was hard enough not to cry on those times it caught him on the back, the legs, or the side of the face. He was wild as a kid, and for that reason, was frequently 'educated' in this way by his old man. But he had no regrets. It was the cruel fire that forged him into this sleek, steel weapon that helped him survive.

Being an undercover drug cop in the North City area was about as suicidal as you can get in St. Louis, and Dagger was good at it. He was the best at being able to take down the gang leaders, as well as the vacant-eyed runners. Sure, he'd been shot at, knifed and nearly beaten to death a few times, but he always gave back more than he got. And the job did have its benefits, including a taxpayer provided Harley to complete his low-life image. Dagger loved his bike more than anything, sitting low to the ground on six hundred pounds of seething, chrome-plated steel, his body vibrating with life, shooting down the asphalt at bone-crushing speed, nothing between him and a fiery death except the strength in his own two arms.

To Dagger, it was like riding a bullet, and he couldn't get enough of it.

But today he wasn't riding a bullet, he was driving a burgundy mini-van back from the most painful experience of his life.

He remembered when he first saw her. Those soft, trusting eyes looking up at him from a pile of filthy rags. Her junkie mother dead on the apartment floor, with a needle still stuck in her arm, her baby's life not even on the same top ten list as the vials of crack in her pocket, or the Dragon Rock crack and heroin combo, which pumped seductive death into her veins. In the center of all this human refuse was this tiny, black-eyed beauty, not even six months-old, cooing contentedly.

The bust was screwed, the perp dead, and the only one Dagger could recite Miranda to was a tiny baby with no one left in the world to care if it lived or died. Dagger picked up the soiled and scrawny infant, and looked at it like it was an annoying piece of evidence he'd have to write up. She looked back at him with those curious eyes, smiled, then spit up on his leather jacket.

From that point on, he was hooked.

He didn't know why he took the abandoned child home, or why he never even mentioned her in his police report. That's what got him kicked off the Somerville Police force. After two months in his home, he decided to come clean and apply for custody.

The pinched-face case worker at the state adoption agency fought hard against Dagger's request. Dagger understood that. He could see her point. He was an authority-hating, unapologetically vicious brute with the most dangerous job in the city...which he had just lost by breaking the law in what could at best be considered a 'compassionate kidnapping.' The people he brought in as character references made the adoption panel break out in visible sweat. On top of that, he had no means of support. All he had to his name was a filthy apartment, a little beer money in the bank, and his precious Harley, which the force let him keep out of gratitude for past services, or fear of asking for it back. There was no wife, girlfriend, or extended family to share the burden of raising a child. He had zero parenting experience, and absolutely nothing to recommend him for adoption. If it hadn't been that absolutely no one else in the world wanted this scrawny, undernourished crack baby, Dagger Lawrence would not be in the position he found himself today.

They celebrated their first official day as a family with a case of Bud and a bottle of formula. He named her Daisy, because that was the name of his first air rifle. She responded by cuddling up in his bulging arms and falling asleep without the slightest hesitation. He could have crushed her in his powerful arms without the slightest effort, but for some reason, that would have been like crushing the life out of his own body. So, after warning her never to spit up on him again, he fell asleep with her, his massive hands protecting her from the coldness of the outside world.

It wasn't easy. He had to put aside money for day-care, learn how to wash another person's bottom, buy a beat-up old sedan, and occasionally bust the face of anyone who dared to say anything sarcastic about him having a black baby.

In return, she taught him how to be yielding in all the places he was rigid, taught him to be patient when he wanted to break something, and taught him that it only hurt a little to tell someone you really love them.

The day she first said "Daddy," he bought a beer for everyone in the auto body shop. The day Daisy started kindergarten, he sat on the floor in the back of the room to make sure her teacher wasn't being too much of a hard-ass. The day she said she wanted ballet lessons, he sold his precious Harley and went shopping for a tutu and tights.

He helped her learn new math by having her teach him what the hell that meant. He gave up completely when she hit algebra. Every report card was mounted proudly on the refrigerator, right next to the Papa John's Pizza magnet. When he caught her shoplifting a candy bar at the local Dairy Mart, he marched her right back up to the confused cashier, then made her admit what she had done and apologize for it. That lesson in morality was complicated when the teenage clerk quickly emptied the cash register, the sight of Dagger stomping up to the counter with a madder-than-hell expression on his face being too much for the pimply-faced teen.

Yet, somehow, they survived those years. The two outcasts, alone and inseparable. He bought her skates, a charm bracelet, and a cheap computer. They learned how to surf the Internet together. When she turned twelve, he had to sit her down on the old worn sofa and explain what happened to ladies once a month, with a face so red and flustered, she laughed out loud, and he had to run from the room in embarrassment.

Somewhere along the line, he went from being 'Daddy' to just 'Dad,' a word usually spoken with eye rolls and the drawn-out inflection of annoyance.

Things were not always perfect. They fought like wildcats, especially because he refused to let her date until she was sixteen. But he never hit her. Not once He would just lift her up in the air, her toes dangling a good three feet above the floor, and he would calmly say; "Now, what is it you want to tell me, little girl?"

He winced, but said nothing when she explained that it was no longer cool for her to be seen in public holding her father's hand.

On her sixteenth birthday, he bought Daisy a frilly dress and a stuffed panda bear, which for some mysterious reason, was the totally wrong thing to do. She ran to her room crying, and he had absolutely no idea why.

She stopped kissing him goodnight after that, and part of him seemed to wither away.

On her first date, he made sure he was in the living room polishing the long, curved blade of his authentic World War II Japanese officer's sword, when the nervous young boy came to the door. In fact, he always seemed to be cleaning some kind of dangerous-looking weapon whenever a boy came to pick up his daughter for a date...something she begged him not to do, but he always did anyway.

He taught her to drive a stick shift in the church parking lot, and they both laughed so hard their cheeks ached.

But today was different.

Today his huge, scarred hands gripped the steering wheel with such fury, his knuckles turned deathly white.

Dagger was alone in the van...so alone, he felt like driving straight into a telephone pole, and letting the van explode in a shower of flames and flying metal.

But he knew he couldn't do that. That live-on-the-edge biker inside him had faded away years ago. She had stolen it from him in unnoticed increments, and he was grateful.

He had to carry on somehow, because Daisy would want him to.

Today was the day he moved Daisy into her dorm room at the Missouri University of Science and Technology. It took less than an hour to move box after box of precious memories out of their old existence and into her new one. She was so excited to begin life on her own, that she hugged him and kissed his cheek and called him 'Daddy' again. She didn't even mind that he hung his over-sized hunting knife on a sheath at his belt, where all those college boys with any smart ideas about touching his daughter would be damned sure to see it.

Now, as he urged the battered old minivan back to his suddenly empty apartment, tears of pride and loneliness streamed down his rough-hewn face.

This wasn't him, Dagger Lawrence told himself repeatedly.

This wasn't like him at all.

THE AFFAIR

With her fragile elegance, sad countenance, and unrelenting gentility, Miss Amelia gave the impression of an old sepia photograph come to life. Hands hidden within lace gloves and skin the color of softly faded ivory, the blush on her cheek was painted now that she peered fearfully from the indiscreet side of fifty. She sat at the quiet, outdoor cafe, perched on the white steel framed furniture as if she were holding court to a throng of unseen admirers. But the imagined throng had been reduced to one; a single young man sharing her glass-topped table, handsome as she could wish, shining a white sculptured smile in her direction. In grateful response, her delicate laughter danced and tickled the air like a lacy Bach melody.

"Oh, you are an evil one!" she whispered amid fluttering lashes. "I can't even pull my hair from my eyes without you labeling it vanity."

His reply was honest, not meant to be offensive.

"Well, perhaps you are right," she continued. "Perhaps I am a touch vain." She angled her smile to perfectly capture the dwindling afternoon light. "Of course, I always believed vanity was a sport which should be played only by those best equipped to endure its rigors."

This time, his words brought a laugh of confident discomfort.

"Vain and elitist?" she gasped with a raised eyebrow. "My, you certainly know how to sweet talk a woman. I do so admire a man who can deliver a devastating compliment."

His simple response strained all laughter from her voice.

"Or truth," she said softly. "Does it matter?" Miss Amelia fidgeted with the cuff of her sleeve, before taking a moment to brighten once again. Her standard play, when in doubt, was a retreat to irrelevance. "I simply can't understand why it has become such a negative thing to be an elitist? I didn't name the masses. They gave themselves that god-awful name. 'The masses.' I would hate to think of myself as some small, ill-defined mass amidst the enormous, amorphous masses."

It was her companion's turn to laugh. He offered her a return dipped in charm, which elicited the desired results.

She gently dabbed a folded corner of a white cloth napkin to her lips, as if to hold back a smile she clearly wanted to be seen. Her voice took on a most musical lilt. "You do make me laugh so. To be honest, I was afraid I had almost forgotten how."

And then she paused, suddenly overtaken by images and voices she dared not reveal. He noticed the downward cast of her eyes, and after a respectful moment, asked about it.

His question seemed to startle her out of her thoughts.

"What?" she asked, followed quickly by, "Oh, nothing. Really, nothing..."

As he pursued, she picked up her crystal goblet of Chardonnay, watched the setting sun set fire to the wine's pale yellow hue, and hid her nervousness within a slow, delicate swallow.

Yet, he would not relent.

"All right," she waved with casually concealed annoyance. "If you must know... For some reason, an old children's story popped into my head. Or part of one, anyway. The past always struggles to intrude at the most inopportune moments."

His answer rang of insincerity, and she told him so.

"Don't be silly. You expect me to believe someone like you would be interested in the ramblings of a crazy, old woman?"

Miss Amelia knew immediately she had committed a tragic breach of etiquette. He recoiled at the reference to the difference in their ages, his eyes flashed darkly at her self-criticism. She hurried to correct her mistake.

"I... I'm sorry... I didn't mean it that way. It just slipped out."

Her eyes flitted down to the lace-covered hands on her lap. "So much for vanity and elitism, I suppose..."

This seemed to satisfy him, and he repeated his question.

There was little else to do. She smiled softly, took in a breath of forced cheerfulness. "Well. If you insist. I believe it went something like this..." Miss Amelia's eyes squeezed shut, as she recited the familiar lines from long ago.

"And all the little Noovogoodlian children crane their long, wire-like necks above the bushes, so as not to be seen seeing that which they should not be seeing, or at least, should not be able to recognize for many years hence."

The ancient rhyme pulled her back and away, his comments of appreciation barely rousing her from her trance.

"Of course, you don't," she recovered with a gentle shake of her head. "I made it up myself."

He was impressed, and quickly told her so.

"Really," she continued. "I used to make up all my own fairy tales. I never could tolerate those age-old standards filled with dumb rams and clever foxes. So, I created my own to entertain the other children."

His return elicited an elegant, well-rehearsed laugh.

"You're right. I admit it. I still thrive on being the center of attention." She ran over his words, coquettish as a kitten. "Well, you *should* feel honored. My old fairy tales are an intimate part of me. It isn't every new acquaintance I allow to view my childhood interiors..." The implication hung in the air.

"As it were."

His response was obvious and appreciated.

"How wicked you can be!" she laughed with delight. "There isn't a single word or phrase I could utter without you twisting it into some fantasy. Some exotic vision where you sweep me off with a flourish, expecting to exact who-knows-what price for your attentions?"

And then the subject was laid on the table before her. She looked away, eyes flitting from the shiny crystal, to the trees ripe with blossoms, and finally to the amused and appalled glances of the other diners surrounding them. Her softened tone denied her words.

"No... No. It doesn't really bother me." She leaned toward him with an earnestness that surprised even her. "Younger men, you see, possess a certain...arrogant grasp on life. Older men let it leak out their pores. Or slowly grow it out of themselves, slicing it off with each whisker they shave, drying up anything left inside with after-shaves that smell of respectability and dotage. You younger men, you wear your life on your chin and upper lip, to show the world you are not afraid to trumpet your virility."

And then the smile returned, as she found herself back on the comfortable ground of feminine playfulness. "Perhaps *virility* is not the kind of word that should come up in a platonic relationship like ours."

She answered his question by nodding to the other patrons without ever releasing his gaze, her voice carefully dressed for seduction. "Because the people at those other tables might get the wrong impression. Believing perhaps, that we may be expressing our affections on more...physical terms. Not understanding that we are both too..." She searched for the perfect word. "...*respectful* of our positions to carry each other off to some erotic playground of soul-searing passion."

Miss Amelia allowed herself another long, lingering sip of wine, underscored with a slightly wicked laugh.

"I always loved the word *'rapture'*, don't you? Just saying the word forces the tongue and lips into such intimate movements...it almost makes a lady blush."

Miss Amelia closed her eyes and softly mouthed the word.

"...*rapture*... I can't imagine any other word in our language that so prepares for the attainment of its meaning...*rapture*..."

A delicate reveal of whitened teeth, her smile grew in response to his widening eyes. "Although, I hear the French language is full of them," she added slyly.

His compliments began to flow more freely now, and she basked in the giddying effect they had on her damaged soul.

"Why, thank you!" she said, as she tossed her hair gently. "It must be you who brings out the poetry in me. I had almost forgotten it existed. My husband says..."

She cut herself short. Quickly attempted to placate the wounded look in his eyes. Her words of apology poured out rapidly. "I'm sorry. I promised never to mention my husband. Only please, let me mention him this once. Then we won't speak of him again...Harold says I have all the melody of a stringless violin. Really. Can you believe he told me that?"

She relaxed, as he gave her the exact answer she wanted to hear. "Thank you. I replied that if he simply tried tuning me more often…rubbed my worn veneer to bring back some former luster, and perhaps put his bow to me with a little regularity, I assured him I could still pour forth a symphony or two. He was not amused."

Although she had long rehearsed this verbal ballet, hidden feelings suddenly pulled the confidence from her expression, and tinted her faltering gaze.

"Take my advice," she muttered, after the briefest of pauses. "Don't ever let yourself grow old on a person. No, I don't mean not to age -- God knows we can never help that. I'm talking about growing *old* on someone."

She gripped the wine glass, drained it in one hard swallow. She stared off at some non-specific point to his right, with words were no longer directed at him.

"You break each other in just to wear each other out. The flesh stays willing, but the spirit grows weak. Love is replaced with habit, devotion with tiring familiarity. First goes the music, then the humor...and all you're left with is the security." She could not hide the trace of bitterness which crept into her voice. "Lifeless, claustrophobic security..."

Her companion stared at her, seeing far more than she had intended him to see. As if awakening, Miss Amelia seemed suddenly aware of the awkward silence which had shrouded their table. She brightened quickly, hoping to distract or avoid his piercing eyes.

"There now. I promise we won't mention him again. However, you must explain that odd look in your eye."

He offered a pleasantry, which neither believed. They had reached the point in this dance where the music was destined to change.

"No," she said tenderly. "The real reason."

He spoke without shame or judgment. His frankness glaring in contrast to her delicately worded minuet.

This time, her blush was genuine.

"Oh...I see," she whispered, unable to look him in the eye, but then she did, with a gaze both pleading and grateful. She moved quickly to calm his fear of having given offense. "No. Not at all. If anything, I'm flattered. After all, look at you... Bursting with such youth and dreams. Exuding such...such..."

She struggled for the right phrase, then stopped. In that moment of discomfort so carefully rehearsed, so desperately dreamed of for months, Miss Amelia suddenly saw the game for what it was, and felt naked before this man. Not sensuous. Just exposed. She let escape the first true and unvarnished smile of the encounter, a smile of resignation.

"Maybe Harold was right," she muttered softly. "Maybe I am just a worn and stringless violin."

Even his kindness could not dispel the glittery mist in her eyes.

"That's sweet. It's such an old line, but it's still sweet. Really it is."

He mistook her epiphany for condescension, and reacted like a hurt child. She almost knocked over her empty glass in a rush to apologize.

"No. Please. I don't doubt your sincerity! If anything, I question mine." She paused to clarify her own jumble of emotions. Honesty gave way to the familiar effectiveness of fluttering eyelashes, and she sighed dramatically to regain composure.

"I'm sorry. I'm not being very fair to you. You've been so kind and attentive. Come on. Smile for me. It becomes you so. That's better... Oh, and that is much better!"

He was past the point of being so easily consoled, and told her so.

"How can you say that?" she asked with more urgency than she wished. "I am not being condescending. That is the total opposite of how I feel. Believe me."

Her heart pounded in her chest, as a dangerous fragility washed over her. The flirtatiousness which had served her well for so many years was slowly losing its hold. She saw his eyes migrate from her to others around the cafe. She knew she was losing him.

Her hands fluttered emphasis like cascades of butterflies. Then fearing the unwanted intimacy they revealed, she abruptly grounded them by her wine glass, then beneath the table, then down to her lap.

This impromptu rendezvous, which she had planned for months, began to slip away from her. The moment had come. Her charade exposed, Miss Amelia leaned across the glass-covered table, and across the three decades that separated them, and surrendered herself to his dark enticing eyes.

She took his hand for the first time. Feeling its strength and heat through lace gloves nearly as old as the trembling fingers they covered.

"You make me feel...," she whispered, her voice hesitant and frightened. "You make me feel as if Harry was wrong. As if I'm not merely a worn and discarded violin. As if...with you...I could get my strings back. For however short a time it may be."

She closed her eyes, refusing to see the pity she feared might move into his.

"And I feel like..."

She had come too far. She had to say it.

"I want..."

She had to let it out, whatever his reaction. The words escaped in a whisper. "I want you to…play me…"

With frightened innocence, Miss Amelia peered up into this handsome stranger's eyes, and was relieved to detect no trace of pity there. She released her glass, and let the young man raise her to her feet, her hand clenched tightly in his. Her face burned with sudden heat and she felt pleasantly disoriented. She let escape a trembling breath, as he dropped a fifty-dollar bill on the table, and then led her silently past the curious and condemning gaze of the other patrons.

His hand fit the small of her back with comforting familiarity. It wasn't until they were almost to his dark green Jaguar, when he spoke again. What he said hit her like a backhand slap. She recoiled, then quickly tried to cover her shock.

"What?"

He explained himself in calm, supporting tones. She nodded, hoping he would not hear the terrible pounding within her chest.

"You, uh…didn't tell me," was all she could mumble.

They stood together by the open door of the Jaguar, and she frantically prayed the tears would not come.

"No. I suppose it doesn't matter," she said, with a staccato breath. "Really, I'm sure."

All her secrets were laid bare before him, as he studied her with detached curiosity. She paused by the open door, felt her eyes drawn to the dark and inviting interior of his vehicle.

A remark, designed to make her feel comfortable, finally shattered the last vestige of her illusions.

Slowly, a sad smile crept over her lips, as for the first time, her voice abandoned all artifice. She gazed up into his face. His so beautiful face.

"Uh, I'm sure there is a less tacky way to ask this," she whispered. "But…do you take checks?"

She nodded softly at his reply.

With a sigh more than thirty years in the making, Miss Amelia let the young stranger ease her into the automobile's dark interior.

He closed the door for her.

Ever the perfect gentleman.

Vanquished

The alluring aroma of sea-tinged air wrapped teasingly around the senses of the young centurion, like the soft, scented scarf of some forgotten lover.

Although he knew he should be concentrating on the task at hand, Nadir Fortuitus was momentarily seduced by a tangled chain of uninvited, impish thoughts, glinting like sunlight through the pastoral splendor of his imagination. Surely, he was not cut out for the soldier's life, a fact he had desperately tried to communicate to his father. Yet, he received only savage looks of proud contempt each time he nervously broached the subject over dinner, or during a non-coital pause in the high season's bacchanal. The legions were in his blood, his father insisted, if not in his heart. Seven successive generations of Fortuitus men had proudly contributed to the inestimable glory of Rome, by breaking the vessels of their bodies, or leaving their life's marks on someone else's spear or swordpoint. His father, red-faced with thwarted persuasion, pounded his remaining fist on the rough-hewn table. Surely there could be no nobler path than being split asunder for a cause as glorious as keeping the Republic whole? Was it not Fortuitus blood which fertilized the Republic and allowed it to grow?! As righteous passion moved the scarred and graying veteran to rise defiantly on his one good leg, Nadir saw his own hidden dreams gradually skewered upon the cold, cruel steel of tradition.

Dreams, his father oft repeated, were merely the bile of undigested responsibility. Yet, dreams, in all their clandestine splendor, were the inviting curse which all but separated Nadir from the noble fate forced upon him.

If it weren't for the sacred blood of his ancestors, he might have been a poet, an architect, or a formidable orator like that cocky Cicero fellow.

Instead, he was forced to trudge the continent under the fierce gaze and inescapable talons of the gilded Roman eagle.

Concentrate. He must concentrate.

Yet, how could he coerce his thoughts to flow along a single narrow trough, when they surged undisciplined, like a joyous, ravaging flood in all directions at once; attacking and overwhelming any pitiful boundaries that Man could erect?

But focus he must. He had a job to do.

His misted eyes hungrily drifted from the harsh iron blueness of the sea, up to the pale blue hue of the sky, then to the painted blue bodies of the wild-eyed Picts, as they crashed and spilled like an enraged wave upon the determined wall of Roman soldiers. As the tepid air filled with shrieks and curses, and his shield buckled under the repeated weight and blows of murderous hate, Nadir Fortuitus thrust forward his spear, and suddenly found he had little difficulty concentrating on the task at hand.

****

The battle with the Pict savages proceeded in the usual manner, which meant the slaughter was choreographed with typical Roman efficiency.

The Picts, like many primitive tribes of the Western frontier, prized individual valor over strategy. Hundreds would rush down the hill, yelping and screeching in an effort to break the courage of their enemy. Their short swords and wooden spears would slash and jab at the closest target, wildly, repeatedly, until either the object of their hate would fall, or the arms wielding their weapons were cut off. The Pict warriors would paint their entire bodies blue in preparation for battle, so the enemy, upon seeing a wave of howling, unnaturally hued figures would believe they were battling something inhuman, perhaps the spirits of the woods themselves.

Much of this was lost on the Roman soldiers, who, in their continent-wide march and long sail across the channel to the Isles of Britain, had seen more than their share of slaughter, repulsed more than their share of desperate charges, and sent more than their share of souls to a thousand primitive gods. The individual valor of the Picts simply fed into the strategy of the Roman legion. The Picts' bloodcurdling shrieks, which could so unnerve the Celts and other tribes, were merely a glorified chorus of war to these battle-tested legions. The blue color just added a little variety to the familiar collage of death, which so added to the glory of Rome.

The Romans displayed their front line in a heavily fortified wedge known as a phalanx. A hundred soldiers would march up a hill, shoulder to shoulder, carrying long iron shields that extended from breastbone to shin. The soldiers were pressed so closely, their shields would snap into place like some great iron wall pressing down on the enemy. Heavy shields, borne by strong Roman biceps, would easily turn aside hurled rocks and the short wooden spears of the Picts. The long Roman spears would insinuate death before the Picts were within sword distance of their enemy.

So savage were the Picts in battle, one man would purposely thrust his body onto a long Roman spear, so that his dead weight would drop the spear to the ground, and hopefully, unbalance the shield holder. Then, another would slice the skull of the spear carrier while his weapon was weighted down with the dying body. This, of course, only worked if you held the advantage of overwhelming numerical superiority, which the tribal Picts seldom possessed by attacking singly, or in small bands.

To Nadir Fortuitus, whose massive arms qualified him for the much envied front row of the phalanx, the battle was noisy but routine. The first surge of blue bodies broke upon the wall, leaving many of their number impaled and dying. The second surge added another fifty or so easy kills. Then, the Picts, realizing distance, not discretion, might in fact, be the better part of valor, lined up just beyond spear length from the Roman front line. They backed up the hill as the wall of eagle-adorned shields continued its irresistible advance. Shrieks and taunts were all they could hurl at the invaders. Still, the Picts huddled and backed up, step by step, in a stubborn, but futile defense of their homes and their lands.

✳✳

Though the battle lasted less than fifty minutes, Nadir Fortuitus was clearly exhausted from another day's work in service to the Senate. Nearly eight hundred blue bodies lie crumpled and severed on the ground. The wounded would be mercifully silenced, less their wails offend the gods' delicate sensibilities. This clean-up action was the chore of the back centuries, since it was largely recognized that the front line had carried the brunt of battle. The Romans had lost twenty-seven men to the Picts' eight hundred, one because he had tripped and inadvertently fallen into a comrade's spear.

Thus, was the glory of Rome preserved.

With the balm of darkness came the traditional Roman pyres, purifying the bodies of slain comrades by fire, and letting the rising ashes carry their spirits to dwell with the gods. The Picts, on the other hand, were left to rot on the ground. Their bodies picked over by scavengers of the night; wolves, buzzards and wild dogs. The sight of hundreds of mutilated corpses littering a field could often persuade unvanquished tribesmen to sue for peace. Some would be angered into further resistance, of course, but their bodies would also serve one day to convince others of Rome's divine right to rule. Anyone who resisted would soon find their blood joining the ambivalent soil.

Although he attended the ceremony with the appropriate solemnity, Nadir Fortuitus did not really believe in the gods. He believed in his dreams, his spear and his shield. These alone defined his existence and encompassed the shifting perimeter of his life. When he died, he knew he would be burned in ritual worship like his fallen comrades in arms, because he had never revealed to another soul his doubt of the gods, and because, well, why take chances, just in case he was wrong. Yet, Nadir was convinced that when he died, he would be as dead as any of the Picts scattered over the ground, who were not allowed into Roman heaven, and were not likely to enter any unsanctioned heaven of their own design.

As his fellow legionaries cast songs both solemn and bawdy into the glowing frenzy of the ceremonial fires, solemn dirges to appease the gods, or bawdy ballads to celebrate the life they had retained, Nadir found himself drawn to the distant music of the sea crashing against the coast. It seemed he alone noticed how the rhythmic pounding of the waves underscored the dire melody of the Roman dirges. Perhaps it was the gods, who may exist in spite of his doubts, providing their own harmony to the ritual music. Or perhaps the earth itself was singing a counterpoint to mock the pitiful dreams of these short-lived, self-important creatures who scurried on its craggy skin like so many bewildered ants.

The earth had cause to mock, for despite wars and shifting boundaries, only the earth was eternal; and men, their borders, their empires and their dreams would soon pass silently away, giving ground like the receding waves, which melt into oblivion as they humbly retreat back into the sea. Men, like the waves, grasp their moment of opportunity to rise up in swaggering glory, and pound on the malleable shore with all the fury they can muster, spread their wet transitory ambitions as far along the beachfront as they can, only to feel the silent pull of future generations, to weaken, draw back, and once spent, retreat into the dark and comforting bosom of mother sea; little more than a glistening moisture in the sand attesting to the dreams they had hoped would last forever, yet even this would be overcome by future assaults on the shore of time.

These were decidedly unRoman thoughts. Musings his father would find frivolous and unworthy.

Romans thought only of empires and eternity. They did not splash on the shore. They marched, like a precision flood, in a well-ordered subjugation of the land. And they believed that what was once in Roman hands would never slip away.

Such will always be the vanity and delusion of conquerors.

Realizing how differently his thoughts were arrayed might have caused despair or dissension in the soul of another man. To Nadir, it brought only peace. He even envisioned his thoughts painted bright blue, doing vain and glorious battle against the world of his father.

He was so cocooned in these thoughts, he did not hear the crushing of a leaf, the movement of an arm, or the heavy wooden branch which kissed his skull with the promise of uninvited oblivion.

✳✳✳

When Nadir finally regained consciousness, pain coursed through his body like so many icy creeks. The realization he was yet alive brought little joy, when punctuated by the guttural language of angry Pict voices. Taken prisoner within a stone's throw of the legion. What would his father say?

Someone must have realized he was awake, because he felt the savage kiss of a rough-hewn knife against his burning throat. Part of him hoped it would bite deep, and return him to the comforting chaos of the abyss.

Instead, a cloth was removed from his eyes. As he blinked back the pain of intrusive light, his eyes filled with the frightening image of...the most beautiful woman he had ever seen.

Her night black hair was wild and energized, framing fierce blue eyes that contained unfathomable libraries of hate and sorrow. Yet every feature, every curve of her translucent face seemed sculpted by the gods as testimony to their preeminent grasp of the absolute. She was wrapped with the hot scent of sweat and femininity, which teased his nostrils with a promise of rapture and destruction. The sudden kick she delivered to his chest only confirmed her status as alluring destroyer.

She was surprisingly strong, and the kick sent him careening backwards against the cold, dank earth. His massive arms were bound from wrist to biceps behind his back. His legs restricted by rough hemp. A long plank punished his spine and limited his movements, so that he could only gaze up at the unconcerned stars from his subjugated position on the ground. Like any good soldier, he did not fear death, just the waste of what might have been, and the softly nagging doubt that he might die for the wrong reasons. But he had little chance to explore these thoughts, as rough hands sat him straight again, the plank in his back pointing skyward, and his field of vision dominated by the fierce countenance of the Pict goddess.

She seemed to be arguing in her primitive tongue with four burly men who clearly felt Nadir should suffer the same unspeakable horrors Rome had exacted from their tribe. A pain for pain repayment in kind. Yet, for all her obvious contempt, there was a sorrowful awareness of the future in her eyes, the realization that her way of life would soon be swept away in the path of advancing Roman ambition. When his eyes met hers, Nadir was overwhelmed with the proud suffering they contained.

He would gladly have fallen on his sword to ease her plight.

This warrior woman, a priestess he surmised, clearly had authority on her side, and the burly men retreated in a grumble of angry deferment. He was left alone with the savage enchantress, hovering between the knife-edge promise of death and enlightenment. Either path would have been acceptable to him.

From the nearby fire, she ladled a strange orange and brown liquid, which bubbled languidly in a primitive iron pot. She chanted for a moment over the steaming spoon and its lugubrious contents, flung her eyes and arms to the stars, and slowly spun three times in a northerly direction. Then she faced her prisoner with all the proud defiance of an unconquerable soul on the moment of surrender. He did not know what to think and began to spout absurd apologies in Latin; sorry I invaded your land, sorry I slaughtered your tribe, sorry I became your enemy, sorry I am a Roman, sorry I am at all; only to be silenced by the flash of anger in her eyes. He knew that his apologies, his words, and perhaps his existence were strangely irrelevant; he must not spoil her ceremony, whatever it entailed.

It all made him feel so terrifyingly alive.

The fierce priestess pushed the steaming spoon of liquid to his lips. Death by poison was not an attractive way to die, but Nadir nodded his acceptance. Oddly, the thick, foul-looking potion smelled of springtime and release, hardly what he had expected. As he painfully, angled his eyes down to the spoon, he dared not guess what the floating chunks in the potion might be. She grabbed his jaw in a firm, yet gentle embrace and pulled open his mouth. He stared in her steel blue eyes and did not resist, even as the hot potion scored his lips and tongue.

The sudden burning sensation was only partially the result of the fire's heat. Immediately, his throat felt ravaged and numb. He could trace the bitter liquid's fiery path down to his stomach, where it burned with even greater intensity. His eyes slowly unfocused and his vision pulsed wildly. The primitive enchantress, so beautiful, so beautiful, smiled at his distress. This vision of her would be a soothing companion on the road to death. Then, to his surprise, she put the ladle to her own lips and finished the contents.

She sat back on the ground facing him, like a dull beetle trying to right itself. Their eyes met and locked, as they drifted together in this unexpected, drug-induced communion.

Nadir felt himself hurled in the air, while being simultaneously slammed deep into the earth itself, as if physical shape and limitation no longer applied. At the same time, he was sucked straight into the priestess' eyes, invaded her skull, swam in the thrilling fire of her bloodstream, danced in the comforting freedom of her soul. They were everywhere at once; on the battlefield, in the trees, in the grave, always together. He felt her presence in every cell of his being, sniffed her warmth and frenzy into his own soul, then forgot he had ever existed without her. There was no Nadir Fortuitus. There was no raven-haired priestess, so beautiful, so beautiful. There was no Roman empire, no Pict hordes, no earth, no day or night. He lived only in her because she was part of him since birth, a birth into timelessness, a birth transcending, a birth which...

And suddenly, without a word spoken between them, he understood the ceremony in all its tragic implications. Why he had been selected, why he had been captured, why she looked at him with that overwhelming sadness which shook his torso like no warrior's blow ever had the strength to do. And he loved her immediately and totally, knowing his life before was forfeit, as was hers, for a higher goal. As they lay writhing in their delirium, four solemn women gently stripped off his clothes and armor, removed her robes, then left them alone on the final step of this odd ritualistic journey to both cheat and surrender to fate. She prepared him in an almost reverential fashion, and he was all supplicating skin and sensations beneath her touch.

As she clung to him with powerful limbs, the purpose of his life, of all life, was suddenly made clear to him, although it would have been impossible to translate into the clumsy mechanics of rough-hewn words and wooden thoughts. As he entered her, he embraced his destiny and felt utter peace with the world for the first, and only time in his life.

****

Three months later, the purpose of their confrontation began to show on her belly. He had not been allowed to meet with the raven-haired priestess again. He spent the long days tied to tree after tree, released only to evacuate his bladder or bowels twice a day. Although they had been separated by the angry tribe, his eyes had a few times met hers from across the camp. And on those precious occasions, those rare, elusive moments which defined his existence, her shy eyes danced with starlight, and spoke to his soul a silent litany only they could understand; for, although he could not yet master their language, he knew her to the very core of her being, and she understood him like no one had ever understood him before. Every moment of his life had been leading up to that mystical, inexplicable journey they had shared, and every moment since merely echoed its loss. Even though he was kept apart from her, bound on the perimeter of the camp, she was ever in his soul.

The tribe had moved steadily northward, avoiding the constant threat of the pursuing Roman legion. A few days earlier, a Roman scouting party had almost discovered their mobile camp, and the burly guard had pushed a sharp-edged knife to Nadir's throat, to keep him from crying out for rescue. But there was no need for the knife; whatever Nadir had been before, he was no longer. He would do nothing to endanger her, even if it meant, as he knew it must, spending his final days bound and tortured.

The purpose of the ceremony had been to create a child; part-Roman, part-Pict, to forestall the inevitable annihilation of their race. Despite their unyielding ferocity, the Picts knew they were a dying breed. Only a new and forbidden intermingling with the blood of their sworn enemy could allow part of their culture to continue in the future. Nadir knew he was merely breeding stock for the high priestess, the Roman half of the equation, and once the child they conceived, during their spiritual reverie so painfully long ago, was born, Nadir would die.

For all his dreams and artistry, he was nothing more than the kidnapped sire of a half-breed king for a doomed people.

And yet, strangely, that was enough.

✳✳

As the months passed, the bound soldier came to understand bits of the crude Pict speech. He learned that the priestess, his priestess, was named Alia, and that she would soon give birth. He also overheard Dorak, the huge, red-headed guard claim the right to slice open Nadir's throat the moment the child uttered its first cry.

The long periods of isolation, not unlike the personal isolation he had felt amidst the crowds of his home town, were not wholly unpleasant for Nadir Fortuitus. For their part, the Pict women kept him fed and healthy, in the event a problem arose with the baby, and he would again have to re-enact the 'ceremony'. Gradually, almost imperceptibly, his identity as a Roman began to feel as painful and binding as the crude ropes which cut daily into his thick wrists.

The summer wind grew stale and chill with the cunning approach of winter. The Picts donned their heaviest fur, and despite grunts of protest from Dorak, Nadir was treated to a warm and comforting deer skin blanket. As the day for the birth fast approached, he caught fewer glimpses of Alia, radiant in her swollen loveliness. She was kept secreted away, in the elaborately painted holy tent, her body ritually cleansed with wild herbs and water, then purified by bitter incense.

Once, in the dead of night, Nadir was awakened by the sound of excited feet and whispered frenzy, but the labor proved false, and the tribe soon returned to its quiet ritual of harvesting, hunting and hiding.

For his part, Dorak enjoyed squatting in front of the burly Roman prisoner and fingering the hungry blade of his dagger, in a gesture only half as menacing as his cold, dead eyes. Although Nadir was far from fluent in the Pict dialect, no words were needed to express the delight the tousled-haired hunter was anticipating from the brief marriage of his eager weapon with the tempting throat of his rival, his captive. The two men, as distant and distinct as the sea and the stars, shared a cruel common language of jealousy and contempt, taught to them by a hypnotic priestess who dominated their thoughts and dreams the further she was removed from their sight. As he fingered his deadly blade, Dorak would stare at his intended victim and harshly whisper one of the few Pict words Nadir could understand...

"Meut."

"Mine."

Then one cold, mocking night, the universe betrayed the small band of ancient warriors. Suckled by the velvet bosom of sleep, Nadir missed the opening screams of charge. His eyes fought their way open in the hypnotic glow of orange rage and the loud assault of Latin curses, like a desperate cry from a half-remembered dream. He saw familiar shields and flashing swords scatter death like poisoned grain among fleeing women and children. The Pict warriors made their valiant stand around the priestess' tent, a frightened human shield against the unrelenting carnage of the Roman scouting party. Although their numbers were roughly equal, the Romans had the element of surprise, which they wielded with deadly precision, slaughtering more than a quarter of the tribe before they could clutch their weapons in twitching, deadened fingers.

As he watched with horror from his perennial position lashed to a tree on the outskirts of camp, Nadir was overcome by an internal battle as fierce as the tumult raging around him. Roman victory meant sweet ransom from certain death, an end to his months of blissful torment and a return to the derisive limbo of his previous existence. He was a man torn between two worlds, two lives, two identities, which now battled hand-to-hand before his terrified gaze.

Nadir tried to stand, scraping the inside of his arms against the bark of the thick tree to which he was continually lashed. Nine of his comrades were leaking their remaining consciousness into the cold, lifeless grass. Nineteen more were slashing and cursing, to ensure his captors did the same. He could count forty-two Pict bodies lying immobile in that peculiar grasping crawl of death and terror. Familiar faces from the past snarled venom at the faces he had come to know during the eight months of his captivity. Dorak's knife, the tool that would end Nadir's life, shrieked blood across the chest of a Roman soldier, and Nadir did not know whether to cheer, or cry out in anguish. Tied to his tree, separated from the battle, was the ultimate torture. He felt he was an observer at the gates of hell, forced to watch the migration of the doomed, powerless to prevent it. Yet, had he freedom of movement and a sword in his hand, on which side would he fight?

The question was answered after a fourteen-minute battle. Most of the Pict tribe had fallen, the rest had scattered to the safety of hills or were taken prisoners. Enjoying the eternal spoils of war, Nadir watched the women who had fed him, being raped by the victorious Roman soldiers. In the midst of one such violent episode, Nadir's eyes connected with the woman who had given him the winter pelt -- eyes that tried hard not to see the conqueror ravaging her body, with lust and hatred.

Finally noticing Nadir tied to the tree, one of the thirteen surviving Roman soldiers drew his short sword to execute the bedraggled savage. But as he approached, Nadir spewed out a stream of coarse Latin bile that widened the soldier's eyes and rocked him back on his unsteady heels.

"Put away your sword, Flavius. You have done enough butchery for tonight."

A full thirty seconds passed before the stunned Roman squealed like a child.

"It's Nadir! Nadir Fortuitus, back from the dead!!"

The reunion was joyful and tragic. He embraced his former comrades as the Pict women watched with deadened, condemning eyes. He felt both betrayer and betrayed, as his friends slapped him on the back and begged to hear his bizarre tale. His only comfort was in not seeing the body of Alia as he subtly scanned the bloody carnage spread below the cold, unforgiving eye of morning.

Nadir drank and laughed with his companions, the Latin tongue like punishing, sharp-edged pebbles in his mouth. He told of his captivity, of Dorak's threats, of the degradation of his status as a Roman citizen.

He did not, would not, tell them anything of Alia, an omission not unnoticed by the silent Pict women.

As he slowly grew reacquainted with the bawdy humor of his friends, he knew his life under the shadow of death was over. And his suffering under the burden of life was beginning anew.

Later, as he toured the captured camp, pretending not to hear the suspicious whispers of his Roman comrades, Nadir averted his eyes from the few living Picts with the strength to raise their heads in silent accusation. He realized he was still wearing the winter deer pelt, and searched desperately for the woman who had wrapped it over his shoulder only days before. He found her on the forest edge of the camp, face down in the sharp-bladed grass, her body already struck cold with death's icy pallor. Hiding a tear of confusion, he draped the animal skin over her unseeing eyes.

Suddenly, there was a feral cry from the bushes. As he turned, he saw red hair, and an equally red face, strangled by rage. Dorak, bloodied and drunk with vengeance, barreled toward his former captive with knife raised, demanding the life of which it had been cheated. To his own surprise, and that of his companions too far away to intercept the sudden onslaught, Nadir Fortuitus made a fatal decision.

He lowered his sword and closed his eyes.

But the dagger never reached his heart. The grunt of pain and surprise he heard did not escape from his own throat, but from that of his attacker.

He opened his eyes to see Dorak, within arm's length, clutching a light spear that protruded through his chest, a look of utter confusion on his face. The huge Pict warrior turned his back on his rival and faced the woods from which the spear was hurled. And his confusion deepened, as did Nadir's, to see a proud Pict priestess, heavy with child, rise defiantly from the bushes.

As Dorak collapsed to the ground, wounded as fatally by the woman's act, as the spear itself, Alia's eyes met Nadir's with a look of haughty defiance. Then, she turned and was absorbed back into the woods.

The next few moments were a blur to Nadir. Two Romans ran toward the trees to intercept the Pict priestess, and the two were almost instantaneously cut down by the angry blade of their former companion. Nadir howled and felled three more of his friends, before lumbering off into the woods in search of the woman who had saved his life in so many ways.

****

Legend has it that the child born half-Roman, half-Pict, became a great warrior king who built an isolated stronghold against both Roman and Celt invaders. His kingdom helped lay the foundation for the eventual civilization of Britain, and his bloodline can be traced to the very flower of European heroism.

Of his star-crossed parents, the priestess and the reborn poet, little is said, except that they lived to a ripe old age, embraced by the forgiving hills of present day Scotland.

Saddest Chicken

"Tomorrow, they are putting me in a nursing home.

Tonight, we're having chicken.

Somehow an entire life of laughter, joy and fear has slipped right past me, marked only by a series of memories too elusive to hold in my swollen hands, and too desperately painful to let go of.

I never knew I could ever get this old. I never knew I could feel this frightened.

I fought against every obstacle, so I could build a life for me and my family. But suddenly, somehow, I became too old to fight.

Too tired to make the choices.

Too lonely to live out my life without someone to need me.

My own children...old enough to know the pain inside me are sitting around the table, trying to pretend that tomorrow is just another day.

But we all know it isn't.

This is the saddest chicken I have ever tasted...."

LAZLO'S MINE

"Look out!" shrieked Linville amid the awful groans and creaking. "She's givin' way! She's...!"

Linville's last words word echoed in a dozen searing, screaming throats, quickly drowned out by the rolling cough of a thousand tons of rock and dust reasserting their position in the earth. The tunnel belched exploding blackness and debris in all directions at once, filling every empty space with suffocating horror.

Fortunately for Linville and the others, their horror was choked off in seconds.

For Webster Corrigan, age twenty-seven, it was just beginning.

He came to a portion of his senses under a crushing blanket of a thick and tangible silence. His soot-crusted eyes could not adjust to the light, because there was none, only a blackness so complete, there was no telling what was one inch, or one hundred feet from his face.

Every part of Corrigan's body screamed in pain, except the blood-soaked left side of his face, and that was something he was too afraid to consider. As his ringing ears strained to the sound of the last few boulders crunching and crushing into place, Corrigan allowed himself a cough, fully aware the betrayal of his own lungs could just as easily trigger another collapse. He hacked fear and soot from deep inside, and spit them back into the darkness.

"Beamis? Linville?"

No reply.

"Rutherford?!" he called softly into the stifling void.

Nothing.

Dead silence, pierced only by his own overly loud heartbeat and ragged breathing.

He dared to whisper a bit louder.

"Morgan?! Potter?!! Oh, please, God...Tell me you're not all dead!"

"...Corrigan...?" The voice seeped through the darkness weak and raspy, but it might well have been the voice of an angel.

"Yeah! It's me! Webster Corrigan! I'm still here! Still alive!"

"Well...ain't that just dandy for you?" came the reply.

That would be Potter. It had to be. Nobody else would be as surly in the middle of a life-threatening disaster.

"Now, can I inconvenience you to quit your bellowin' long enough to git these damn planks off'un my legs?!" That was Potter all right. The man's crustiness knew no bounds.

"Where you at, Potter?"

"You still got a workin' flashlight, boy?"

"Yes, sir."

"Well now might be a right clever time to use it."

Corrigan silently cursed himself for not thinking of the flashlight on his belt straight off, but there was something about a mine disaster that flung logic to all corners of the skull. He muttered a silent prayer as he reached for the thick metal handle, then slowly traced his fingers up to the recessed button. The powerful beam tore through his eyesight as painfully as it ripped the smothering void.

"Damn, that's bright!"

"We consider that a good thing, Corrigan," smirked the voice from the far murkiness. "Now shine it over here, ya durn fool...!"

The beam of light scratched the blackness, until it discovered the coal-smeared face of the old miner. Everyone knew Potter was on the crotchety side of fifty-five, but with the sweat and grime seeping into each crevice of his pain-contorted face, he looked as old as the earth itself. The stab of illumination traced down from his squinting eyes to the three heavy wooden beams that covered his body from the waist down.

"Jesus, Sam... your legs..." Corrigan gasped.

"Yeah... They's busted all to hell. ..." Potter winced. "Just my luck. I was supposed to take the old lady dancing come Saturday night."

"Jesus, Sam..."

"You said that. Only I'd rather you picked up those planks than go and say it again."

"Uh...sorry. I'll get it."

"Real gentle-like. Any big moves could have this whole section crumbling down around our ears again."

As if in answer to the old miner's warning, the mine's bones let out another creak and shudder, spitting spidery showers of coal dust around the frightened men. Both Potter and Corrigan froze, waiting to see if the dust would be followed by something deadlier. When the creaking stopped, they each breathed a sigh approaching, but not nearly, relief.

"I reckon we might be okay for a while," Potter whispered. "But I suggest you don't go takin' the Lord's name in vain no more, leastways not as long as we're in this particular situation were in. If you git my meanin'."

"Okay, Sam," Corrigan nodded. He gently placed the flashlight on a jutting rock and aimed it toward the injured man. He wrestled nausea and panic back down to his gut, then stooped to move the massive wooden beams. They were heavier than they looked. Old wood from the early days of the mine. The splintered beams tore at his fingers; his lungs filled with dust as he tried to raise a corner with every effort he could muster. His arm and back muscles shrieked with exertion, and Potter shouted with pain.

"Arrrrrgggh!"

"Does it hurt, Sam?"

"No, you idiot." Potter gasped. "I'm auditionin' for the Grand Ol' Opry! 'Course it hurts! It hurts like hell!"

"I'm sorry, Sam."

Potter sucked in a few ragged breaths to regain his composure. "Okay. Apologizin' for stupid questions is a good thing," he said, through gritted teeth. "Stayin' alive is a good thing, too,"

With gut-wrenching exertion, Corrigan finally shoved and slid the three damaging planks aside. With what seemed like equal effort, Potter slowly wedged his mangled frame up to a seated position; his back pinned against a large rock protrusion, his crumpled and useless legs stretched in odd angles before him. He spat out a low grumble of curses at the shredded limbs which had carried him for so many years into the gaping holes of the earth; now little more than two splintered fragments among the rubble, pieces of human debris blending into the wreckage of rock and wood.

Neither man spoke for a long while; Corrigan unable to look at the older man's shattered legs, Potter unable to look away.

As if emerging from a trance, Potter suddenly groped through the shadows until his fingers felt the familiar lip of his miner's helmet. He placed the hard hat above his brow, finding comfort in its familiar pressure, and then switched on the small battery powered light attached to its front. By turning his head, he could now chase the gathering shadows from whatever section of rock fell prey to his nervous gaze.

Not knowing what else to say, Corrigan asked, "Where are the others? Beamis and Rutherford and all?"

Potter's voice was hard as granite, as he scanned the stone ceiling for the next potential weak point. "Beamis and Rutherford and Morgan were tryin' to scramble out of Section 247, last I heard."

"Jesus, Sam. Section 247 was one of the worst hit! If they was in there when it let go, then they're sure to be..."

Potter's fierce glare swung from the rock wall to Corrigan's face, where it struck cold and corrosive as a rusty drill bit. "You think I don't know that, Corrigan?!" he spat. "You think I don't know what fifty tons of falling rock can do to a man's skull? You think I don't know there won't be enough left of those poor bastards to scrape outta there?! Huh?!"

"Sorry, Sam..." Corrigan mumbled. "Just weren't sure you knew, is all."

"Well, I *do* know! I do know. Lord help me, I know at least three friends of mine are dead because the damn coal company pushed us too far, too deep and too fast. I know that everything from 311 to 247 behind us is under more'n a mile of dirt and rock. And I also figure everything from 241 to daylight is sealed off in front of us."

"Ya think?"

Potter's gaze lost its focus, but none of its bitterness. "And I know all that means we're about as screwed as two livin' men can get."

"You think we're trapped down here?"

In response, Potter pointed his helmet light straight into the younger man's eyes. He let it hang there without saying a word.

"I... I'm sorry, Sam..."

"Apologizin' for stupidity is good, Corrigan. But I'm losing my patience for it real quick-like." Potter scanned the walls again, aware of how the light only pushed back the edge of the darkness, which bore back down on them every time the weakening beam moved aside. "Hell, these things happen every twenny years or so," he sighed with forced casualness. "We was just unlucky enough to be the ones down here when the whole kit 'n caboodle collapsed."

Corrigan nodded. It was luck. Bad luck. Nothing more. "I heard tales," he said. "Lots of tales about this kinda thing... But I never thought it would happen to me."

"Nobody does, Corrigan. If I'da knowed it was gonna happen, I'da prob'ly called in sick today myself."

"I guess."

Potter eyed Corrigan carefully, as he tried to size up the frightened young man who shared this isolated pit of destruction. He had heard enough tales to know a panicked miner could be just as deadly as carbon gas during a cave-in, and he intended to have none of that. "Jus' you stay sharp, boy. I ain't got no patience for any hysterics. You hear me?"

Corrigan nodded grimly. He had heard the same stories.

"I hear you, Sam... I ain't gonna go 'round the bend on you."

The fear in the young miner's voice stung Potter nearly as much as his mangled legs, the legs he was rapidly losing feeling in, even when he tried unsuccessfully, to shift positions. All he got for his efforts was a sprinkle of coal dust and a frightening lack of breath. The old miner snorted and pursed his lips. "Hell, we're still alive. That's a good thing." He paused, before adding, "If they can open up a passage, we just might make it outta this mine alive."

"Ya think?"

This time the pause was less natural, a teetering stone above the two men neither wished to acknowledge.

Silence.

Then more silence.

"I was in one of these before, ya know." Potter finally said, if only to break the oppressive quiet. "About twenny years back, over in Milton County. They put some durn fool kid with three months' experience blasting a whole new section of the mine. It weren't hard to figure out what was gonna happen. The kid used too much dynamite and placed it in the wrongest possible spot. He shouts "Fire in the hole!" and there's this big deep rumbly boom. I could tell by the way the ground shook under my feet that somethin' was wrong. Real wrong. But I was young and stupid...funny how those two always go hand in hand...." He shook his head, lowered his eyes to the cave floor. "So I just walked straight into that mine as soon as they gave the all-clear."

Potter waited so long to continue the story, Corrigan was afraid the injured miner had lost consciousness. Just as he was about to prod the old man, Potter's voice rose again, only this time it was eerie and distant, like it rose up from a part of him that wasn't more than half alive.

"That shaft was sneaky as mines can be. It waited about forty-five minutes before it decided to get pissed. Then, that whole mine just sorta belched and shuddered and closed its dark, angry mouth on near to fifty-three good men. Fifty-three good men..." He shook his head again. "When the rescuers finally burrowed out a hole, I was the only one they pulled out alive."

Corrigan couldn't think of anything to say.

"Alive is good," he mumbled helpfully.

"Sometimes it is... Sometimes it ain't," Potter shrugged, his squinty gaze fixed years behind the darkness which entombed them now. "For months, I had to look at the teary faces of all those new widow-women. Look in the eyes of all those kids suddenly without a daddy. Look in all those faces, and not be able to tell them why I made it outta that mine, but their husbands and daddies didn't."

"Well, Sam, I'd sure as hell rather do that, than end up under a big pile of rocks."

"Tell me that again in three months, Corrigan." The old miner's piercing steel eyes shot back at Corrigan. "Three months... That's all I could stay in that there town, afore I up and moved down here to Lazlo's Mine."

Corrigan squatted down on a pile of rubble by Potter's twisted limbs. He never would have gotten this close to a senior digger before, but there is a democracy in disaster, which all miners understood. "When I get outa here, Sam, I'm givin' up minin' for good. I ain't never livin' through this again."

"We ain't lived through this one yet, kid."

The two men grew still, as that thought sunk deep into their bones. Potter grabbed a small piece of hard shiny coal from the mine floor, and twirled it in his fingers. In the silence that followed, Corrigan stood and began to pace, his dimming flashlight darted about the rock in a frantic attempt to find some sudden opening they had somehow overlooked.

"How long you reckon afore they send a rescue crew down here, Sam?"

"Depends on whether they think we're alive or dead." Potter spoke to the hard lump of coal in his gnarled fingers. "If they think we're goners, they just might blast a new hole. That could make the rest of these walls collapse." He snorted softy. "They could rescue us to death, Corrigan. Sorta ironic, don't ya think?"

"No, I don't think it's ironic!" Corrigan coughed out a mouthful of black saliva. "It's real damn pitiful, if you ask me!"

"Then I better be sure not to ask you," Potter said gently. "Besides, if the fallin' rock, or lack of air don't kill us, the gas surely will."

Another pause. Corrigan's eyes flew from rock to shadow to solid desperation. His heart was pounding louder now; unbearably loud.

"You smell the gas, Sam? Think gas is seepin' in here?! Man alive, that'd be all we need!"

"You never smell the gas, Corrigan. It ain't got no smell. It just makes you drowsy-like, and before you know it, you're sleeping your way to eternity."

"I don't wanna die like this, Sam!" Tears streamed down the young miner's cheek, creating small black streams, like finger-tracings of death on his face.

"Seems to me like we ain't got a whole lot of choice in that matter. Old Lazlo's Mine done had its say, and our arguing about it ain't gonna amount to nothin'. That's just the business, Corrigan. Every miner who ever walked all blustery proud into Lazlo's mouth knew there was a better'n even chance this kinda thing would happen someday. And every night we walked out at the end of a shift, we knew we beat this cantankerous old mine one more time. If we walked out on our own two legs, we won."

Potter dragged a grimy paw across his tired eyes, and wondered whether it was the gas making it so hard to focus.

"Only this time, it looks like the mine won," he muttered without emotion.

Corrigan could take no more. He stood over the old digger, his boots grinding deep and wide into the dirt. "How can you be so damn calm, old man?! We're gonna die in here! You know that?! We're gonna die in here!"

"Maybe…" Corrigan looked up at him sharply. "But the more you panic, the harder you struggle against those rocks, the more oxygen you use up. That kills us both. Best to sit down, be still and wait it out."

"Not me! I ain't gonna roll over and die like some damn…some damn bug! I'm finding me a way outta this hellhole!"

"Suit yourself. Send me a postcard if you git the time."

"You're a mean old bastard, Sam Potter. You know that?"

"Never claimed to be any different. Too bad you cain't choose your dyin' companions, ain't it, Corrigan?"

Corrigan glared at the crippled man with pure hatred that shone through the darkness like no artificial light could ever do. Then, he turned on his boot heel and retreated into the shadows.

"You lay down here and die if you have a mind to, Potter! I'm gonna see if there's an opening in 243. Maybe I can dig us a way out." The hard echo of his retreating footsteps soon lost under the creaks and moans of unstable earth.

"You do that, Corrigan," the old digger whispered to the darkness. "You do that."

Alone in the gloom, Samuel Potter picked up the lump of hard coal again. "It's a damn, pitiful shame, it is." He said to the rock, as he held it close to his craggy face. "All my life…just rootin' underground for you…a piece o' rock-like crap that's stupid enough to burn." He chuckled without mirth. "And the durndest thing is that in fifty million years or so, with enough pressure from all this rock, I ain't gonna be nothing more than a lump of coal like you. Then some poor bastard futuristic miner is gonna be diggin' me up!" His hoarse laughter caused him to wince, the pain slowly returning to his shattered legs. "Hell, in fifty million years they probably won't even burn coal no more… Probably just be using some kinda renewable energy by then. No poor bastard is gonna have to sell his soul to this here darkness anymore, just to feed his family. No-sir-ee."

A stabbing agony gnawed its way up his torso. His breath shortened in defense, and his elbows pressed tightly to his ribs in a vain attempt to push back the fierce spasms.

"Yeah… Workin' in the sun's the way it oughta be… The way it oughta be, I tell you…"

As minutes turned into hours, or maybe even days — it being so hard to tell in a mine - his helmet lamp flickered and slowly died out. The ultimate insult.

Alone in the black void, Samuel Potter, senior digger, company man for more than thirty-nine years, slowly realized the terribly small dimensions of his universe. The suffocating darkness pressed in on him, heavy and immovable as the rock walls that defined his existence, and his body began to shake uncontrollably. This is how a coffin feels, his mind screamed at him, only worse.

But worse.

So much worse.

The yell that tore from his throat echoed against the shifting dirt above, sending torrents of petal-soft blackness to mingle with his terror.

"I don't want to die down here!!" he cried to whoever or whatever could hear him. "I don't want to die in the dark like some animal! I don't want to die!"

He groped for his face, unable to even see his hands pressed against his eyelids. He knew tears alone could not wash away a lifetime of soot and false bravado, but he didn't care anymore. All he wanted was a chance to see light. Warm, sweet light. He swore to God and to the mine and to the bodies of his dead partners, he would never take it for granted again, the way those who have never plumbed the bones of the earth take light for granted. And through his coal-streaked tears he could almost visualize the light, coming forward, seeking him out, welcoming him home...

"Sam?"

It was Corrigan. The kid. Shining his weakening flashlight in his face. Watching the lifelong dirt-crawler sobbing like a baby.

"You okay, Sam?"

Potter dragged a sleeve across his face. "What the hell you lookin' at, Corrigan?! Get that light off me! You come back to gloat or somethin'?"

Corrigan's voice was soft and frightened. "No, Sam. I ain't come back to gloat."

Potter tried to pull himself together. The scared look in the young miner's eyes hurt worse than his legs. "Ain't you found a path to China yet?"

"No, Sam. I tried every which way I could. It's sealed tight as a tomb back there."

Potter's tears dried up, inside and out. "Good analogy, Corrigan," was all he could mumble.

Corrigan set himself down by Potter's feet. He searched the old man's face, found at last the desperate humanity they shared.

"But I can hear them, Sam. They're comin' for us."

Potter's expression was too hopeful. "You better not be joshing me, boy."

"No, Sam," Corrigan said gently. "I can hear them. I think they're close."

His eyes blurred by the first effects of the poisonous gas, Samuel Potter strained his ears to the darkness.

"I don't hear a durn thing, Corrigan..."

Webster Corrigan placed a comforting hand on the older man's shoulder. "They's out there, Sam," he whispered softly. "They's coming for us..."

"Ya think?"

"You lie back and sleep, Sam... I'll do the listenin' for both of us."

"You can really hear them, Corrigan?"

"Yeah, Sam. Just listen..."

Ignoring the creaking of the mine, Samuel Potter closed his eyes to catch fleeting visions of familiar faces and green trees shining in the sunlight.

"They're out there, Sam..." Webster Corrigan whispered from somewhere farther and farther away.

"Just listen..."

THEIR FATE

As they shuffled and awed from piece to piece, the undulating stream of art critics and cultural potentates who descended on Beningworth Gallery reminded Wallace Alexander Bonica of a plague of locusts, with their incessant chirping and the way they devoured the emotional balance he had tried to build into each work. He watched them ingest his art, corrupt it with the acidic juices of their own internal agenda, and noisily excrete their lofty interpretations with lifeless eloquence.

Art imitates life. Criticism imitates understanding.

In the view of the world-famous sculptor, neither is especially good at the task.

Perhaps it was because the consensus on Wallace Alexander Bonica's latest exhibit was far less clear than in previous years. A few called it inspired, but a larger number labeled the exhibit a self-conscious betrayal of the artist's own distinctive style. The artist himself, clinging to corners with ears tuned to the incessant buzz of pretension, was impressed with how elegantly one could politely disembowel another's creative soul.

Perhaps Wallace Alexander Bonica had visited such criticism upon himself, as the madman who dashes into a field during a thunderstorm and hurls challenges at the arcs of divine vengeance must claim partial responsibility for the lightning bolt. It was no accident of fleeting inspiration which drove him to divorce a style of sculpture which had proven internationally popular, but was no longer personally satisfying. His hands could easily have fashioned as before, but his heart held them back. A fever, seven months in the making, had corrupted his ability to compromise; poisoned his inner well of self-disdain. It was an infection of hope, which can be a deadly affliction in an industry which values cynicism and societal loathing above all; his new sculptures shocked the traditional art patrons by unashamedly oozing with optimism.

Unlike the petty disseminations of his life, the sculptor had found a way to carve pure romance.

If the affront to his own artistic style wasn't enough, the mode of its expression was equally crude. This was not his traditional champagne-reinforced gala opening on Fifth Avenue, a glittering social event listed on all the right calendars, with a limited number of private invitations sought after like water in the Sahara, or respect in a junior high locker room. For nearly two decades, that had been Wallace Alexander Bonica's preferred unveiling; the elegant social strata arriving meticulously attired and exquisitely coifed to confront his offensively primitive works of tortured passion.

Much to the chagrin of Maurice, his agent of the past twelve years, Wallace had insisted on opening his new collection in this tiny gallery plunked down in the worst possible part of town for a social event. The hall even had a carpeted floor!

The gaunt agent had alternately begged, threatened, pleaded and cajoled, but to no avail; the artist as set in stone as his works. Wallace Alexander Bonica steadfastly refused to exhibit anywhere but the Beningworth Gallery on Lower 14th Street; and worst of all, in Maurice's opinion, gave no hint of the dramatic change in his style which he would not allow anyone, not even his agent, to witness until tonight's unveiling. Maurice entered the gallery expecting easy sales of derivative Bonica pieces, and was instead taken aback by sculptures as foreign to him as NASCAR graffiti.

The work was good, that was understood by all. But an agent doesn't sell good, he sells recognizable, and this new work sprung from a Wallace Alexander Bonica he did not know.

He heard the hush of the crowd and imagined it underscored by the tight slamming of fat checkbooks. In short, Maurice saw all the warning signs of artistic meltdown, a phenomenon of the truly inspired, those talented few who create daring works in obscurity, catapult to fame, and then begin to impetuously believe the press releases about their enduring brilliance. This phenomenon was best epitomized in Nobel Prize-winning playwright Samuel Beckett's 35-second long work entitled *Breath*, in which an audience sits for just over half a minute as the theater lights come up on a stage full of debris, then slowly fade while ethereal offstage moans of some theoretically symbolical significance are heard.

Maurice was afraid he had another Beckett on his hands.

He couldn't have been more wrong.

Although the new work was nearly the antithesis of the Wallace Alexander Bonica style, its mastery of stone, clay and ceramic touched something deeper. The raw materials of the earth glistened with a new sensitivity that assaulted the very concept of the inorganic; for surely in these pieces, so lovingly wrought, life was wrung from lifelessness, and arias coaxed from the inanimate. Those sophisticates who had come seeking the usual feral expression of a Bonica work, were confronted with a tender realism and subtlety of form which brought to mind the loving hand of ancient Roman masterpieces, with marble kissed and beguiled by the chisel to reveal a skin smoother than any fabric, softer than any smile. And smiles there were, for these became the subject of much of the exhibit. Smiles and eyes, and most of all hands, gentle hands touching hearts, touching arms or merely touching air with unearthly grace. The forty-seven pieces represented a woman broken into parts, but somehow made more gloriously complete by the artist's loving examination of each individual feature.

The masterwork at the center of the gallery was a massive, mixed-marble sculpture, seven feet high, illustrating the tender intersection of two forearms. One, rough-hewn, imperfect in color and form, suggested a man's arms with desperate fingers extended in confusion. Yet, on it rested the whispery touch of a woman's hand; willowy smooth, in flawless white marble; the hand of a goddess, with tragically expressive fingers resting lightly on the man's forearm. Where they intersected, the woman's enticing caress had the effect of making the rough and primitive arm softer, smoother, as if her touch alone brought peace to the anguished limb; an emotional Midas changing whatever she touched to tranquility instead of gold.

The two components in this masterwork were joined by a metal pin hidden so perfectly, the male and female arms seemed to dance separately in mid-air, brushing together as lightly as the wind.

The nameplate on the piece was simply titled, *Her Touch*.

Wallace Alexander Bonica had first envisioned this sculpture while in a hallucinogenic stupor lying in a clinic not far from this gallery, where he had undergone emergency treatment for a massive gastrointestinal infection. Food poisoning run rampant. The attending physician assured the fevered patient that he would have died had he not been dumped, half-delirious, at the door of the clinic by a Turkish cabby who did not even know the victim's name.

During eleven incoherent days, Wallace Alexander Bonica clung not to life, but to a vision; an ethereal reflection of a woman who, with a single touch, had reached through the fog of his life to find a soul drowning in ambivalence and self-contempt. Gradually, the infection diminished, while the vision only became stronger. He moved from the clinic to a hospital emergency room to Intensive Care to a standard patient room, and she was always with him, though never in physical form. He took with him her eyes, her hair, the curve of her cheek, the line of her smile, the hue of her skin, and most of all, the sensual image of her hand on his arm. These pieces of her became more tangible to him than the hospital bed, the smell of disinfectants the parade of faceless nurses, or the creek of antibiotics and saline which slowly ebbed life back into his veins.

He remembered her only in bits, but those fragments had somehow made him whole again.

It was on the eleventh day that Maurice finally found him, and insisted on his release. The frightened agent had arranged a private care facility set up in the artist's spacious loft. Maurice had arrived at Wallace's apartment two days earlier, only to find the door open and nearly a million dollars' worth of sculptures in shards on the floor. Five pre-teen vandals were quickly apprehended, but could shed no light on the whereabouts of the famed artist. After a desperate search, the agent finally found his client listed as John Doe in the indigent care ward of a downtown hospital. During those two days of panic, Maurice had come to realize the true depth of his relationship with the missing artist, an insight which annoyed him to no end.

Although the doctor suggested a full month of rest and recuperation, Wallace ordered Maurice to discharge the nurse in his loft, and immediately began work on the imposing marble sculpture which now dominated the gallery. He worked days and nights, sleeping only when he could no longer hold the chisel, eating only enough to add strength to his hammer blows. He accepted no calls and would let no one enter, accept the fast food delivery boys who were greeted roughly, tipped well, and immediately dismissed. Then he would once more pour his entire essence into the marble, never caring if there was enough left to sustain him.

And for once in his life, Wallace Alexander Bonica felt like a true artist.

****

Rebecca Matheson turned her scratchy wool collar to the evening chill, as she crossed the remaining two blocks to the subway station. She walked without purpose, allowing her feet to follow the familiar path of their own volition; for purpose was something which had long ago disappeared from her life. She had her work, of course, and her house, as well as a massive black cavity in her chest where her dreams lay dormant.

Oddly enough, dreams were easier now that Greg had left her, no longer even a specter in her life.

As cliché as it was, her husband decided a selfie on a dating app was more real to him than the woman he actually married; the mere fact he had never met her added lubricant to his ability to communicate at the deepest and most personal levels. Through the unseen interplay of binary numbers, he came to know this stranger's thoughts and hopes and fears and desires, while Rebecca came to know only his increasingly sullen moods and apathy.

Five months later, she found a yellow Post-It note attached to her bathroom mirror.

> *Bec,*
> *I'm leaving. We both know why.*
> *Keep the house and everything else. I'm taking only the old Chevy*
>
> *and the computer.*
> *Sorry I was never able to make you happy.*
> *Greg*

And so, a marriage unraveled without complaint, and with only minimal regret. Even the king-sized bed felt less cold in his absence. Even though she hated herself for not missing him as she felt she should, Rebecca could not deny the cruel vacuum of what he represented, which was the prospect, however dim, that one day they might have discovered what went wrong; one day they might have had the courage to acknowledge their fears and their flaws; and that one day she might even have known the sublime and elusive pleasure of sharing total intimacy with another living soul.

Instead, she walked through her days alone, with only the hope of years, not the hope of life. She felt she was merely counting the days until she died, not with fear as much as gray acceptance. She knew she had no interest in replacing Greg with another sterile relationship.

She did not need marriage, no longer believing in the cruel illusion of love everlasting.

Sex would come when she was ready.

Her soulmate never would.

She was content to fill her last months with dull, desiccating routine. Moved through a daily rotation of work, home, sleep and work again, as if in a trance, a body only, a heart disengaged; unconsciously absorbing only those sensory impulses she needed to survive.

That night, she heard the masked footfalls in the alley to her right and her body recoiled, but did not fear. An icy breeze grabbed her chest, and she pulled her coat tightly closed, but refused to hurry her steps. She took in the visual details of the stoplight, the potholes, the subway entrance, and the large poster of the art exhibit across the street, but did not take the time to acknowledge the familiar look of the artist.

Nor the pleading in his eyes.

****

The opening gala was drawing to a close, as Wallace Alexander Bonica pressed his back to the wall with disappointment. He was not disappointed over the bidding, because Maurice, in his usual spontaneous panache, had convinced many wealthy art investors this new direction in the famed sculptor's work would only make his early pieces far more valuable. In this way, the gaunt agent found a home for all remaining unpurchased works which could be identified as coming from Bonica's pre-romantic period. Of the new sculptures, a few small sales were made, mostly to women, who seemed enchanted by this new romanticism, and told him so with leering enthusiasm; gushing invitations to which the once promiscuous artist remained strangely unresponsive.

The largest bids had centered around the seven-foot masterwork, the caressing marble arms which dominated the exhibit. Yet, to Maurice's renewed exasperation, the artist had declared the work not-for-sale. Of course, this only escalated the ferocity of the auction to seven-figure bids, but Wallace would not be moved. It was a gift, he told the stunned audience of admirers, but would not say to whom. A number of blushes on fair cheeks, revealed that many women who had previously slept with the temperamental sculptor secretly believed it might be for them. That perhaps they had touched the legendary artist on such a profound level, as to have him dedicate this embodiment of quiet passion to them. Many of these women stayed late into the evening, but seeing themselves unrecognized by the increasingly distant look in the artist's eyes, eventually gave up hope of being the recipient of such a stunning gift.

****

She gazed at the white marble profile in silent awe and, at the same time, winced with sorrowful recognition.

She absorbed the soft curve under the eye, the slight crinkle of the lips, and it shook her from the inside out.

She moved slowly from piece to piece. Entranced by the artistry and the warmth it conveyed. Humbled by this shrine of devotion and intimacy.

Love incarnate, she thought tragically. *More feeling in stone than I have left in my soul.*

When she stood before the massive intertwined arms soaring through the air, the masterwork of Wallace Alexander Bonica, she gasped out loud.

She could not help herself. She had to reach out to it, touch the smooth marble hand with her own fingers, trace its sensuality and the ardor of the artist it reflected.

She reached out, but was immediately rebuffed by a painfully thin man in an expensive teal suit.

"Please, do not touch the artwork!" the man snapped with a tone of dignified outrage.

Rebecca Matheson, 42, looked up at the man with his cold, disdainful eyes and suddenly felt an inexplicable need to cry. She pulled her hand back quickly, and began to mutter a stream of pitiable apologies, which seemed to draw only more contempt from the tall man.

"This is a private showing. May I see your invitation?" he asked imperiously.

She didn't have one, of course.

She hadn't meant to stumble into this gallery.

She didn't know anything about art.

She just wanted a momentary escape from the night chill.

Blushing with embarrassment, Rebecca Matheson shook her head and turned to leave, only to find her path blocked by another figure, a face from a distant memory, with eyes that ignited a part of her she thought was dead.

"It's all right, Maurice," Wallace Alexander Bonica said softly to his agent.

He gently reached out his hand to her and said, "She's with me."

And from that moment on…

…she was.

WISDOM

"What you lookin' at?

Didn't your meemaw ever learn you that it ain't polite to stare? I should know. I sit in this old rocking chair on this here porch all day, starin' at folks.

But I'm old and I can do that. They always let old folk get away with things other folk can't.

Come up here, and sit with me a spell. I know, you young folk is always in a rush...rushin' off to your meetings and heart attacks and ulcers and all. But when you is my age, you'll greatly appreciate someone ploppin' down in a chair beside you, if only for a spell.

That's right. Make yourself comfortable. Lord knows I do. Sometimes comfortable's all you got left, so's you might as well snuggle up to it.

Now don't go gettin' the idea I'm one of them kindly old biddies. No, sir. I don't have me a whole lot of years left, and I ain't gonna waste 'em bein' somebody's idea of what some sugar-coated old Granny should be. Not me.

Y'see...back when I was a baby, all wild and free, my Pappy said I was stubborner 'en a mule. And Pappy was right. I always had a mind to do things my own way. The way I figgered it, if God didn't want us to use our own heads, He wouldn't a placed them on the top of our bodies. Least that's the way I see it. Lord knows I gave my Pappy fits, and if it weren't for Momma always taking up for me, I wouldn't a had a stitch of skin left on my backside a'tall. I was stubborn, all right.

When I became a new bride way back in 1923, my Lambert swore I was the most pig-headed woman in all of Mississippi. An' he was probably right. I always done things my own way. Still do.

Lambert, he just sorta shook his head and tol'rated me the best he could. It weren't easy for him, Lambert being a prideful man and not used to having some little bit of a thing not doin' what he says. But he was a good man, as husbands go. I guess I gave Lambert a run for his money, but he was always fair to me. Yes, he was. He never raised a hand to me, even when I sassed him like no wife ever should. I reckon I made him laugh, and that's why he put up with me so long. He may've called me the most pig-headed woman in all of Mississippi, but he done said it with a smile.

When my Lambert up and died on me, and left me on my own with five hungry young'uns, I was even more of a spitfire. Folks around town called me 'willful and ornery,' 'specially when I wouldn't take no new husband to help raise my babies.

Finally, when time whopped me up the side of the head, and made me an old woman, people started callin' me 'feisty,' 'cuz Lord knows I was too set in my ways by then. Now that I'm ninety-four, they say I'm eccentric.

Eccentric...

I can be meaner 'en a snake, or crazy as a loon, and they just shake their heads and whisper, "Don't worry none 'bout Old Bessie. She's just eccentric, is all."

Heh heh...I get away with murder now.

That's what I call progress!

No need to get up outa that chair yet. I can fit more plenty more words into this visit. Looks like it's goin' to be another hot one today. You might as well set a spell longer. I sure could use the company.

You're not from around these parts, are you?

That's a shame. There's somethin' mighty precious about this here land. Families sink their roots way down deep into this soil. It nourishes 'em and helps 'em grow strong 'n close. Old Miss is family country, don't you know. When your eyes get as old and sharp as mine, you can see it in the grass, the way each blade bends under the footsteps of so many generations. When your ears get as old and clear as mine, you can hear it in the wind...the way babies cry and their mamas coo and cuddle 'em to sleep on a hot summer night. The church bells, singin' right out and proud...

Did you know we got us more churches in the South than 'bout anywhere else in the whole United States of America? This is God's country, sure enough. And He watches over us. He's prob'ly sittin' up in heaven right now, watchin' you watchin' me. Yup... He's just sittin' there contemplatin' how much longer He gonna keep me on this here porch, before He decide to take me up to be with Him and Jesus and Lambert and all my five babies.

Bless 'em. Bless 'em all...

Yeah, they's all with Jesus...but let's not talk none about that. I done say everything there is to say to 'em every mornin' I wake up alone in this old shack. There ain't no more words to tell on the subject of a parent outlivin' her own babies. Ain't no more words to tell. Only tears.

Only tears...

But enough about that. They's in a better place than you 'n me.

You a Christian? That's a shame.

Well, I suppose God made some people He had to convince along the way. If you got a mind to, go see Pastor Winfrey down the road apiece. He'll set you straight. And you tell him Old Bessie sent you. I keep that man in business, don't you know.

Yes, I do.

You know, a lot of folk say some terrible things about the Old South. They laugh and say we's backwards, 'cuz we talk slow and move at a more leisurely pace than you Northerners. But let me set you straight on somethin'. Talkin' fast don't mean your brain is keepin' pace with your tongue. I know whole lots of Yankees whose tongues start waggin' and who's brain ain't even in the race!

They don't unnerstand that we in the South talk slow and move slow 'cuz we mean to enjoy this beautiful old world the Good Lord saw fit to hand us. Why rush through it and make your last days come any faster? Don't make no sense to me. But, what do I know? I'm just some crazy, old black woman on her front porch.

No... wait there a minute, now I'm an African-American. I almost forgot. I'm a crazy old African-American woman sittin' and rockin' on her front porch.

In my ninety-four years on Earth, I been a darky, a colored, a Negro, a black, and now an African-American. My best friend Elizabeth went from bein' a cracker to a honky to a...I don't know what else. She's real jealous, 'cuz she's ninety-five and ain't had near as many names as I had.

I believe Elizabeth is gettin' real eccentric...

You know what I think? Names are just silly words our ears use to get in the way of our eyes. All those things I been called ain't never made one lick of difference 'bout who I am inside here.

They's just names, is all. I'm still me.

Elizabeth, she lives in that shack just over yonder. She and I was talkin' the other day 'bout the way folks think they know all about you, just 'cuz they give you a certain name. I'm old. I'm black. I'm a Southerner. But, Mister, you don't know me at all, 'til you spent some time sittin' on this here porch, seein' the things I seen, and livin' the things I done lived through.

Maybe, if you do all that, then you'd come to know a little of what's in Old Bessie's heart.

Now I know you gotta rush off, but let me say one more thing 'bout the South before I shut my mouth up...

The South, it ain't just old ways and hot weather. It ain't about Confederate prejudices and redneck ways. It ain't even the new skyscrapers and fancy jobs movin' in to all our big cities nowadays...

The beauty of this here land lies in the people who walk it... Folks who ain't afraid to be what they is, and say what they believe, even when it's tougher than molasses to swallow straight. We're hard down here...stubborn, prideful, and maybe even a might bit eccentric.

But we can live with that, mister.

We can live with that.

Well, you just go on about your business now. If you have a mind to, come stop by my front porch 'nother day.

I'll be sittin' here in this old rocker.

I'm always here."

Next Chapter...

Now you got me lying here
thinking about you lying there
thinking about me.

And then thinking how I'd be lying to myself,
if I wasn't thinking about lying right there
next to you

right now…

About The Author

Vin Morreale, Jr. is an award-winning author, screenwriter, acting teacher and internationally produced playwright.

He was awarded the prestigious *Al Smith Writing Fellowship*, and his scripts, stage plays, documentaries, museum exhibits and radio comedy have received hundreds of productions around the world, and have been translated into multiple languages, including Chinese, Italian, Russian and Spanish.

Vin has sold material to network and cable television networks, had feature screenplays optioned and produced, and his work has been seen on screen, stage or print in more than 15 countries around the globe. He was recently named a top screenwriter by both The International Screenwriters Association and The Blacklist.org.

Vin was a founding member of the San Francisco Playwrights Center and the Senseless Bickering Comedy Theatre. His book on theater, *BURNING UP THE STAGE: Monologues, Short Scenes & Audition Pieces for Actors From Six To Seventy* is distributed worldwide through Dramatic Publishing, which also carries a number of his published plays.